LTL
12|14

Looking at her had become an exercise in torture.

He wanted her. Plain and simple. Whether that want would go away after a few hours of fun—as usually happened—he couldn't be sure. This wanting, the one keeping him up at night, felt different. Rooted. Like it wouldn't die with fast, primal sex.

What he didn't need was a woman getting inside his head and staying there. His adult existence had consisted of the hunt to find his mother's killer. It was, in fact, all he knew—emotionally speaking. He had no room for anything else. No room. Zero.

When he found the killer, maybe then. Now? No way. He'd blow off his own head trying to juggle a relationship with his mom's case.

But Jenna was looking at him with those amazing blue eyes and that punch to the chest ripped his air away.

Hell with it.

D0957869

THE MARSHAL

USA TODAY Bestselling Author

ADRIENNE GIORDANO

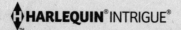

HARLEQUIN® INTRIGUE®

If you purchased this book without a cover you should be aware
that this book is stolen property. It was reported as "unsold and
destroyed" to the publisher, and neither the author nor the
publisher has received any payment for this "stripped book."

For those who've known personal tragedy
and understand that the heart never forgets.

Recycling programs
for this product may
not exist in your area.

ISBN-13: 978-0-373-69810-3

The Marshal

Copyright © 2015 by Adrienne Giordano

All rights reserved. Except for use in any review, the reproduction or
utilization of this work in whole or in part in any form by any electronic,
mechanical or other means, now known or hereinafter invented, including
xerography, photocopying and recording, or in any information storage
or retrieval system, is forbidden without the written permission of the
publisher, Harlequin Enterprises Limited, 225 Duncan Mill Road,
Don Mills, Ontario M3B 3K9, Canada.

This is a work of fiction. Names, characters, places and incidents are
either the product of the author's imagination or are used fictitiously,
and any resemblance to actual persons, living or dead, business
establishments, events or locales is entirely coincidental.

This edition published by arrangement with Harlequin Books S.A.

For questions and comments about the quality of this book,
please contact us at CustomerService@Harlequin.com.

® and TM are trademarks of Harlequin Enterprises Limited or its
corporate affiliates. Trademarks indicated with ® are registered in the
United States Patent and Trademark Office, the Canadian Intellectual
Property Office and in other countries.

Printed in U.S.A.

Adrienne Giordano, a *USA TODAY* bestselling author, writes romantic suspense and mystery. She is a Jersey girl at heart, but now lives in the Midwest with her workaholic husband, sports obsessed son and Buddy the wheaten terrorist (terrier). For more information on Adrienne's books please visit adriennegiordano.com or download the Adrienne Giordano app. For information on Adrienne's street team, go to facebook.com/groups/DangerousDarlings.

Books by Adrienne Giordano

Harlequin Intrigue

The Prosecutor
The Defender
The Marshal

CAST OF CHARACTERS

Brent Thompson—A protective and loyal deputy US marshal trying to solve his mother's twenty-three-year-old murder case.

Jenna Hayward—Former beauty queen turned private detective who works for Hennings & Solomon and has been asked to assist Brent on his mother's cold case.

Penny Hennings—A sassy Chicago defense attorney and Jenna's boss at Hennings & Solomon.

Special Agent Russell "Russ" Voight—FBI agent who is also Penny's boyfriend and a friend of Brent's. Russ assists Jenna and Brent in the investigation.

Aunt Sylvie—Brent's mother's sister. She lived next door when the murder occurred and became the mother figure in Brent's life.

Jamie—Brent's older cousin and another protective female in his life after his mother's death.

Uncle Herb—Sylvie's husband and Jamie's father. Uncle Herb became a father figure to Brent after his father moved away.

Sheriff Barnes—Sheriff in Carlisle, Illinois, who was the first responder the night Brent's mother died.

Mason Thompson—Brent's father and a suspect in his wife's murder.

Terrence Jeffries—A drug addict who lived in Carlisle and was a suspect in the murder.

Chapter One

This was a switch.

Deputy US marshal Brent Thompson stood in a Chicago hotel ballroom among a throng of impeccably dressed political big shots that, for once, he didn't have to protect.

Tonight he was a guest.

Whether that made him happy or not was anyone's guess. But he'd stay another hour for Judge Kline, a woman he'd spent two years watching over after her husband and children were murdered by some nut who'd been on the losing end of a ruling. Judge Kline had ordered him to pay a $1,200 fine and somehow he was mad enough to wipe out her entire family, leaving her to deal with guilt and rage and heartache.

Crazy.

Sometimes—*sometimes? Really?*—Brent didn't understand people. Or maybe it was their motivations he didn't understand, but the human race baffled him.

Tonight Judge Kline, who'd refused to allow her life to collapse under grief, was smiling. A welcome sight since her eighty-five-year-old mother had decided to throw one hell of a shindig for the judge's sixtieth birthday.

"Brent?"

Brent turned and found the ever-polished Gerald Hennings, Chicago's highest-profile defense attorney, weaving

through the crowd. Accompanying him was a petite blonde
in a floor-length bright blue gown. She had to be over fifty,
but may have had a little work done to preserve her extraordinary looks. Her perfect cheekbones, the big blue eyes and
sculpted nose were duplicates of the ones Brent recognized
from Hennings's daughter, Penny. Didn't take a genius to
figure out this woman was Mrs. Hennings. Brent held his
hand out. "Mr. Hennings. Nice to see you."

Five months earlier, Brent had been assigned to protect
Penny Hennings after yet another nut—plenty of nuts in his
world—had attempted to kill her on the steps of a federal
courthouse. Penny had nearly put Brent into a psych ward
with her relentless mouthiness and aggressive attitude, but
he'd formed a bond with her. A kinship. And, much like
Judge Kline, they'd remained friends after his assignment
had ended. For whatever reason, emotionally speaking, he
couldn't let either one of them go. The fact that they'd all
experienced tragedy might be the common denominator,
but he chose not to think too hard about it. What was the
point? None of them would ever fully recover from their
individual experiences. All they could do was move on.

Hennings turned to the woman at his side. "I don't think
you've met my wife, Pamela. Pam, this is Marshal Brent
Thompson. He was *the* marshal."

She smiled and—yep—he was looking at Penny in
twenty-five years.

"I know," Mrs. Hennings said. She stepped forward and
gripped both of his arms. "Thank you."

The gesture, so direct and heartfelt, caught him sideways and he stiffened. Freak that he was, he'd never gotten comfortable with strange women touching him. Most
guys would love it. Brent? He liked his space being his.

But he stood there, allowing Penny's mother to thank
him in probably the only way she knew how. He could go on
about how he'd just been doing his job, which was all true,

but even he understood that he'd worked a little harder for Penny. She reminded him too much of his younger sister, Camille, and he hadn't been able to help himself. "You're welcome. Your daughter has become a good friend. And if I ever need legal advice, I know who to call."

Mrs. Hennings laughed.

Mr. Hennings swooped his finger in the air. "You're not working tonight?"

"No, sir. Judge Kline is a friend."

"How nice," Mrs. Hennings said.

"Yes, ma'am. I worked with her for two years. She would always tell me if my tie didn't match. That happened a *lot*."

"As the mother of two sons, I'm sure your mother appreciates that."

Mother.

Mr. Hennings cleared his throat and, in Brent's mind, the room fell silent. He glanced around, looking for...what? Confirmation that the room at large wasn't listening to his conversation?

Maybe.

All around people gabbed and mingled and pretty much ignored Brent. *Imagined it.* He exhaled and once again the orchestra music—something classical—replaced the fog in his brain.

He'd fielded comments about his mother almost his entire life. It should have been easier by now.

Except for the nagging.

Twenty-three years of gut-twisting, anger-fueled obsession that kept him prisoner. "My mother died when I was five, ma'am."

Social pro that she must have been, considering her husband's wizardry with the press, Mrs. Hennings barely reacted. "I'm so sorry." She turned to Gerald, shooting him the stink-eye. "I didn't know."

Moments like these, a guy had to step up and help his

brother-in-arms. "No need to apologize. I think about her every day." And knowing how this conversation would go, the curiosity that came with why and how such a young woman had died, Brent let it fly. "She was murdered."

Social pro or not, Mrs. Hennings gasped. "How horrible."

Brent sipped his club soda, gave the room another glance and came back to Mrs. Hennings. "My sister and I adjusted. We have a supportive family."

"I hope they caught the person who did this."

"No, ma'am. It's still an open case."

A case that lived and breathed with him and had driven him into law enforcement. If the Carlisle sheriff's office couldn't find his mother's killer, he'd do it himself.

"Are the police still looking into it?"

Brent shrugged. "If they get a tip or some new information. I work it on my downtime, but downtime is short."

Mrs. Hennings, obviously still embarrassed by bringing up the subject of his dead mother, turned to her husband. "Can't one of your investigators help? You do all sorts of pro bono work for clients. Why not this?"

"Pam, those are cases where we're defending people. This is different."

Brent held up his hand As much as he'd like help, he didn't want a domestic war started over it. "Mrs. Hennings, it's okay. But thank you."

Still, down deep, Brent wanted to find the person who'd wrecked his family and had saddled him with a level of responsibility—and guilt—no five-year-old should have known. Every day, the questions haunted him. Could he have helped her? Should he have done something when he first heard a noise? Was he a crummy investigator because all these years later he still couldn't give his mother justice?

At this point, if he couldn't find this monster on his own,

he'd take whatever help available. Ego aside, justice for his mother was what mattered.

Mrs. Hennings kept her gaze on her husband. "You were just complaining that Jenna is bored with her current assignments. After what Brent did for Penny, give Jenna his mother's case to investigate. It'll challenge her and keep her out of your hair. Where's the problem?"

Mr. Hennings pressed his lips together and a minuscule, seriously minuscule, part of Brent pitied the man. If he didn't agree with his wife, his life would be a pile of manure.

Mrs. Hennings shot her husband a meat cleaver of a look, then turned back to Brent. "My husband will call you about this tomorrow. How's that?"

With limited options, and being more than a little afraid to argue because, hey, he was no dummy either, he grinned at Mr. Hennings. "That'd be great. Thank you."

JENNA SLID ONTO one of the worn black vinyl bar stools at Freddie's Tap House, a mostly empty shot-and-a-beer joint on the North Side of Chicago.

How the place stayed in business, she had no idea. On this Wednesday night the sports bar down the block was packed, while the only people patronizing Freddie's were an elderly man sitting at the bar and a couple huddled at a table in the back.

The bartender glanced down the bar at her and wandered over. "Evening. Get you something?"

You sure can.

"Whatever's on tap. Thanks."

He nodded and scooped a glass from behind the bar, pouring a draft as he eyed her black blazer and the plunging neckline on her cashmere sweater. "Haven't seen you in here before. New in town?"

As much as she'd tried to dress down with jeans, she

hadn't been able to resist the sweater. When dealing with men, a little help from her feminine wiles—also known as her boobs—never hurt. "Nope. New in here, though."

"You look more Tiffany's than Freddie's."

Already Jenna liked him. "Are you Freddie?"

"Junior."

"Sorry?"

"Freddie Junior. My dad is Freddie. I took over when he retired."

He slid the beer in front of Jenna. Once more she looked around, took in the polished, worn wood of the bar, the six tables along the wall and the line of empty bar stools.

"Slow night," Freddie said.

Lucky me. She opened her purse, pulled out a fifty and set it on the bar. Next came the photo taken the week prior by a patron in this very bar. He glanced down at the fifty, then at the photo.

"I'm not a cop," Jenna said. "I'm an investigator working for a law firm."

"Okay."

She pointed at the photo of two men with a woman in the background. Jenna needed to find that woman. "Have you seen her in here?"

He picked up the photo and studied it. "Yeah. Couple of times. When a woman like that walks into a beer joint, there's generally a reason. Kinda like you."

Figuring it was time to put her cleavage to work, Jenna inched forward, gave him a view of the girls beneath that V-neck and smiled. Most women would love the idea that a fifteen-pound weight gain had gone straight to their chest. Jenna supposed it hadn't hurt her ability to claw information from men—and maybe she used it to her advantage. But she also wanted to be recognized for extracting the information and not for the way she'd done it.

Did that even make sense? She wasn't sure anymore.

All she knew was her need for positive reinforcement had led her to using her looks to achieve her goals. That meant wearing clingy, revealing clothing. Such a cliché. But the thing about clichés was they worked.

"Any idea what her reason for being here was?"

Freddie took the boob-bait and leaned in. "No. Both times she met someone. Why?"

All Jenna could hope was he'd gotten the woman's name. "My client is being held on a robbery charge. He says he was in here the night of the robbery and he met this woman. Her name is Robin."

"Where'd you get the picture?"

"Friends of my client."

He dropped the picture on the bar and tapped it. "Birthday party, right?"

"Yes. My client and six of his friends. Any idea where I can find her?"

"Nah."

"Did she pay by credit card?"

If she paid by credit card, there would be a record of the transaction, and Jenna would dig into the Hennings & Solomon coffers and pay Freddie a high, negotiated sum for a look at his credit card receipts. From there, she'd get a name and two calls later would have an address for Robin-the-mystery-woman.

"Cash."

Shoot.

Freddie may have been lying. Jenna studied him, took in his direct gaze. Not lying. At least she didn't think so. Again with the wavering? Didn't she have a good sense about these things? Yes, she did. For that reason she'd go with the theory that Freddie seemed to be a small-business owner who wanted to stay out of trouble while trying to make a living. She dug her card and a pen out of her purse, wrote her cell number on the card and placed it next to the fifty on the bar.

"How about I leave you my card? If she comes in again and you call me, there's a hundred bucks in it for you."

Freddie glanced at the card. After a moment, he half shrugged. "Sure. If I see her."

Jenna took one last sip of her beer, slid off the stool and hitched her purse onto her shoulder. "Thanks." She nodded toward the fifty. "Keep the change."

Chapter Two

At 9:00 a.m. the following morning, Jenna stepped into the Hennings & Solomon boardroom and found her boss, the man known around Chicago as the Dapper Defense Lawyer—Dapper DL for short—sitting at the end of the table. Not a surprise since he'd called this impromptu meeting by sending her a text at 7:00 a.m.

Not that she minded the text. When that happened, it meant he needed help, and that little boost—that feeling of being the one that Gerald Hennings, defense lawyer of all defense lawyers, called on—never got old. From the beginning, he'd had faith in her. Even when her application to the FBI had been denied and she'd taken a job at a PI firm as their quasi receptionist-turned-investigator, he'd seen potential and had hired her as one of his two full-time investigators. She'd always be grateful for the opportunity to prove herself.

She'd also be grateful that he'd never—not once—hit on her. Most men did. Simple fact. As a former Miss Illinois runner-up, part of her success came from men wanting to sleep with her. And, let's face it, some men were idiots. When those idiots wanted to seduce a woman, they started talking.

A lot.

"Sorry for the sudden meeting," Mr. Hennings said.

"No problem, sir."

Given his choice of the conference room rather than his office, she assumed others would be joining them and took a seat two chairs down.

Penny Hennings, Gerald's daughter and a crack defense attorney herself, swung in, her petite body moving fast as usual. "Sorry I'm late."

She hustled around the table and took the seat next to her father. The guys around the office secretly joked about the killer combo of Penny's sweet looks and caustic mouth. A viper wrapped in a doll's body.

"You're not late," Mr. Hennings said. "Relax."

"Hi, Jenna." Penny high-fived her across the table. "I love these unscheduled meetings. It's always something juicy."

Mr. Hennings smirked. "Don't get ahead of yourself. It's not a client."

Penny made a pouty face. "Boo-hiss, Dad."

The boss laughed and shook his head at his daughter. "I ran into Brent Thompson at a function last night."

Now that got Jenna's attention. She'd worked with Brent briefly. He'd been assigned to protect Penny from a psycho who'd tried to blackmail her into throwing a case. Each time Jenna had locked eyes with the studly marshal, her blood had gone more than a little warm. He had a way about him. Tough, in charge and majorly hot.

"Really?" Penny said as if the idea of her father and Brent running in the same social circles was ridiculous. "*You* ran into Brent? Was he working?"

"No. He was a guest at Judge Kline's birthday party. Apparently he was one of the marshals assigned to her after her family was murdered."

"Huh. I had no idea. That man is full of surprises."

"We got to talking about his mother."

For whatever reason, Penny's eyebrows hitched. *"Really."*

Jenna cocked her head. "That's the second time you've said 'really.' What about his mother?"

Still focused on her father, Penny ignored the question. "He doesn't usually talk about her. I don't know the whole story. He mentioned it to Russ, and Russ told me."

Russ—Penny's FBI agent boyfriend-soon-to-be-fiancé, if Penny had anything to do with it—was a great source of information, and Jenna had learned to use him sparingly, but thoroughly. "What about Brent's mother?"

Mr. Hennings turned to Jenna. "She was murdered twenty-three years ago."

Frigid stabs shot up Jenna's neck. If her boss wanted shock factor, he'd succeeded. "Wow."

Penny glanced across the table. Momentarily stymied, Jenna gave her the *help-me* look. "The case is still open," Penny said.

Her father turned back to Jenna. "You've indicated you'd like more challenging work."

Despite her temporary paralysis, Jenna sensed an opportunity coming her way. "Yes, sir."

"You know what they say about being careful what you wish for."

"Sir?"

"Brent's mother's case, it's cold. My wife has gotten it into her head that we should have our investigators work it."

Jenna sucked in air. A cold case. Simply amazing. For months she'd been craving something more than paper trails and fraud cases. Something she could tear apart and hone her skills on. But this? Could she handle a murder? If it were here in the city, she might be able to pull it off. Her list of contacts was growing, and her retired detective father still had people who owed him favors.

"Hang on," Penny said.

Yes, hang on. "Did the murder happen here?"

Penny threw up her hand. "Hang. *On.* Dad, I'll do anything for Brent, but we're attorneys. This case has no defendant. Therefore, no client. How do we do this if there's no client?"

"It's pro bono."

Penny dropped her head an inch. "I'm… Wait… I'm confused. Again, no client. How are we working pro bono if there's no client?"

"We're helping a friend. I'm not sure how we'll do the paperwork. There may not *be* any paperwork. I really don't know. All I know is that your mother had that look about her."

Penny sat back and sighed. "I know that look."

Jenna raised her hand. "Where did the murder happen?"

"Carlisle, Illinois," Mr. Hennings said. "About sixty miles south of here."

Oh, no. She had zero contacts that far away. Even Russ probably wouldn't be able to help her. Although, maybe he knew someone who knew someone. Heck, maybe *she* knew someone who knew someone.

"You're hesitating. I assumed you'd be interested."

"I am. Interested."

I think. Breaking a cold case would send her value on the professional front soaring. A cold case would prove she had skills beyond her looks.

Still with her hands folded, Jenna took a minute to absorb it all. Twenty-three-year-old murder. Sixty miles away. No contacts. Juggling it with other cases. *Piece of cake.* Hysteria cramped her throat. *I can do this.* She inhaled, straightened her shoulders and channeled Jenna-the-lioness, the Jenna everyone around the office knew.

"I can handle it, sir. Thank you."

"Good. Penny is your point person on this." He turned to Penny. "You're the logical choice. I can't give it to one of the associates. Technically, this case doesn't exist. Plus, he's your friend."

Jenna flipped her thumbs up. This was a chance to have a profound impact on someone's life. "Works for me. Let's solve a cold case."

"GOOD MORNING, MARSHAL THOMPSON," Penny Hennings said in the snarky voice that had earned her the Killer Cupcake moniker from law enforcement guys who'd been on the rough end of one of her cross-examinations.

Brent stepped into the Hennings & Solomon conference room—a place he'd been countless times before—and smiled. "Good morning, *Ms.* Hennings," he shot back in a damned good imitation.

Penny popped out of her chair, cornered the huge table and charged him.

He held his arms out and folded her into them. "You're like a teeny-tiny bird," he cracked.

She gave him a squeeze, then shoved him back. "Well, I was going to be nice, but now I'm not." He unleashed a teasing smile and she rolled her eyes. "Don't think that smile will work on me," she said with sisterly affection. "I'm a lawyer. I'm *immune*."

"Yes," came a female voice from the end of the table. "But I may not be."

He'd know that voice anywhere. Jenna. Five months ago he'd been standing in the hallway right outside this room and spotted her amazing body gliding toward him in a way that would make any red-blooded male drop to his knees. He'd seen her dozens of times since then, and she'd invaded his mind on a regular basis. She was one of those women lucky enough to have her weight evenly distributed, but with a little extra magically landing in all the right places. With her long legs—perfect for a guy who clocked in just shy of six-four—and a body that was more lush than slim, Jenna Hayward gave him an itch he seriously wanted to scratch.

Right now, though, he needed fresh eyes on his mother's case, and his mother always took precedence.

He held his breath, readying himself for the sight of Jenna to knock him daffy. By now he knew to prepare for it. That first day? He'd been toast. He released his breath, turned and there she was, sitting with her shoulders back and one hand resting on the tabletop. Her long dark hair fell over her shoulders and draped over her red blouse. The blouse with one more button undone than was technically appropriate. He studied that extra button and imagined…

Don't.

He brought up his eyes and found her staring at him, head tilted. Their gazes held for a long second, the blue of her eyes sparking at him and—*yeah, baby*—he started to sweat. Slowly, knowing exactly where his mind had gone, her lips eased into a smile that should have dropped him like a solid right hook. *Bam!*

"Nice to see you, Jenna," he said.

Very nice.

She stood and he moved to the end of the table, holding out his hand. She took it, gave it a firm but brief shake. "Hello, Brent. Always a pleasure."

"It's like a reunion in here," Penny said.

Penny. Right. They had company. He unbuttoned his suit jacket and took the seat across from Jenna, leaving the head of the table open for Penny. Her meeting, her power spot.

He waited for Penny to get settled and then angled toward her. "Thank you for doing this."

"It's the least we can do. You know I hate to get mushy, but you mean a lot to us. If we can help you get some kind of closure, we'll do it."

Brent slid his gaze to Jenna. Talking details about his

mom in front of people he barely knew never came easy. The basic stuff about her murder and the case still being open, he'd gotten used to. Now he'd have to get comfortable with Jenna real quick. And not in the way he wanted.

He swiveled his chair to face her. "Are you sure you want to do this? It's been twenty-three years. The case is as cold as they get."

"I don't mind a challenge, and if we can figure this out, well, I suppose we'd all be…satisfied."

"I'd be more than satisfied. But listen, there's no pressure here. If you can dig up some leads, it'll help. A fresh look might crack it."

"Maybe," Jenna said.

"Where do we start?" Penny asked.

"I can tell you what I know, take you to the crime scene, go over whatever notes I have. The sheriff is a good guy. I can't see him being subversive. Right now, he's got an unsolved murder messing with his violent crime statistics."

Jenna's eyebrows hit her hairline. Yeah, that statistics line sounded harsh. *He* sounded harsh. After spending eighty percent of his life wondering what happened to his mother, he'd forced himself to detach. Emotional survival meant burying the pain. Stuffing it away.

Coping 101. Brent style.

The phone at his waist buzzed. "Excuse me, I need to check this."

Text from his boss. They had a tip on a federal fugitive. He shot a text back, stood and buttoned his flapping suit jacket. "Ladies, I'm sorry. I need to go. Jenna, call me with your schedule. Outside of work, I'm at your disposal."

She gave him that slow smile again—simply wicked—and his chest pinged. Son of a gun. In a matter of minutes, she'd figured out how to distract him from thoughts of his mother.

Whether that was good or bad, they'd soon find out.

THAT EVENING JENNA rode shotgun in Brent's SUV while they drove the sixty miles south to Carlisle, Illinois, a place so foreign to city girl Jenna that she wasn't sure she'd even speak the same language.

Maybe that was a tad extreme, but Brent had exited the tollway and immediately engulfed them in miles and miles of farmland. Could she get a Starbucks? A Mickey D's? Anything commercial?

Not even six o'clock and the late October sky suddenly had gone black. She smacked her legal pad against her lap. Marshal Hottie had taken off his suit jacket and rolled his shirtsleeves a few times. The slightly messy look fit him. The suit look fit him, too. He was one of those men who could wear anything and still look good. Not fussy, pulled-together good, but rugged good.

She smacked her pad against her leg again and he glanced down at the offending noise before going back to the road. The man had an amazing profile. Strong. Angled. Determined. Even the bump in his nose added to his I'm-in-charge persona. She'd like to see his hair—those fabulous honey-brown strands—a little longer, but he was working the short, lawman look nicely.

"I'm not great with sitting," she said.

"Not the worst thing. We're only five minutes out."

"Can you give me a quick overview? Are you okay with that? I don't want to upset you while you're driving."

"Jenna, it's been twenty-three years. If I need to, I can recite the facts of my mom's case in my sleep."

"I guess after a while it becomes…what? Rote?" *Ugh. What a thing to say.* "Wait. No. Bad word choice. I'm so sorry."

Brent shifted in his seat, switched hands on the wheel. "First thing, you've got to get over that."

"What?"

"Worrying about offending me. I'm fairly unoffendable.

And when it comes to my mom, if finding her killer means dealing with you speaking freely, I'm on board. Do your thing, Jenna. Don't get hung up on my emotions. If it's too much, I'll remove myself and let you work. I need you focused on my mom, not me. Got it?"

Well, hello, big boy. "I sure do."

"Good. I called the sheriff this morning and let him know we were coming. He'll meet us at the house—the crime scene—so you can take a look."

Jenna jotted notes. "This is the house you grew up in?"

"Yes. My father still owns it."

"Does he live there?"

"No. He's off the grid. Haven't seen or heard from him in nine years."

She stopped jotting. "What's that about?"

"Wish I knew. When I was in college, he paid off the house and left me in charge of Camille, my then seventeen-year-old sister. I was on a football scholarship and had to figure out how to stay in school, play ball and get my sister through high school. My aunt and uncle lived next door so they helped until Camille graduated and went to college. Now she lives in the city with her newly acquired husband."

And, wow, Marshal Brent was a machine with the way he recited his life history. "Who lives in the house?"

Brent cleared his throat. "We lived in it until Camille left for college and I could afford to move to the city. Now it's empty. It'll stay that way until we figure out who killed my mother. I pay all the bills and the house needs major work, but I don't want anything painted or repaired. There might still be evidence somewhere."

In an odd way, it made sense. Who knew the secrets buried in the floors and walls? Any major construction would wash away potential evidence. "I understand. It's smart. And amazing that you've maintained the house on your own."

Not to mention the fact that at nineteen, an age when most young men were focused solely on the number of women they could sleep with, he'd managed to help raise his younger sister. "Your dad, is he a...um..."

"Suspect? Yes. The husband always gets a look. They haven't been able to clear him." She tapped her pen and Brent glanced at her. "Get over this hesitation, Jenna. I need you unfiltered and open-minded."

Sideways in her seat, she focused on him. She couldn't quite grasp his he-man attitude. Sure, he had the physical size of a tough guy, but even the most hardened men had to feel something when their mother had been murdered.

But he wanted unfiltered. She'd give it to him. "Tell me what happened."

A corner of his mouth lifted and hello again, Marshal Hottie.

"Atta, girl. It was just after midnight and we were sleeping in our rooms. I woke up to a noise in the living room—I'd later find out it was my mother hitting the floor after someone blasted her on the skull. We never found a weapon."

Jenna jotted notes in her quasi shorthand, but paused to look at him. His features were relaxed, as if he was deep in thought, but other than that, she sensed no anxiety. They might as well have been out for a Sunday drive given his body language.

"I heard the back door shut. I figured it was my dad coming home. He worked second shift at a manufacturing plant. Farming equipment. But the house got quiet. Usually, when my dad came home, he walked straight back to their bedroom and the floorboards squeaked. That night? No squeak. I stayed in bed for a few minutes thinking about it, and then got up to look."

"Were you scared?"

"No. I don't know why. I should have been."

Jenna took notes, letting him focus on the road and on the facts of his mother's murder. Facts she was stunned he remembered with such clarity and, again, recited rather… dispassionately. He hooked a left onto another rural road and pressed the gas. *What speed limit sign?* "You left your room?"

"I walked down the hall to the living room and found her on the floor." He tapped the top of his forehead. "Bleeding. Then I got scared. My mom's sister and her husband live next door and I ran there. My uncle went back to check on her. He called 9-1-1 from the kitchen phone, grabbed my sister and brought her to be with me. My aunt and uncle put us in their bed and told us to go back to sleep. By then, I was too scared to do anything so I stayed there." He glanced at Jenna and then back at the road. "I can't figure out if that's a blessing or a curse."

"Probably both."

"Finally," Brent said. "She's unfiltered. That's what we need. For twenty-three years the same man has had this case. He's done a decent job, but he only sees what he sees."

Just ahead, a crossing came into view. To the right, a few houses with lit windows dotted the two-lane road. Brent cruised past them and continued on for a quarter mile to a second set of twin, single-story homes with cute porches she'd bet were great for sitting on during summer. One house was dark, the other with only a porch light. He pulled into the driveway of the darkened one, parked and cut the engine.

"This is it," he said. "If my aunt and uncle are home, they'll be over in three minutes. Guaranteed."

Jenna sat forward, scrunched her nose at the darkness. "I'm assuming the electricity is on."

"It's on. We've got ten minutes before the sheriff arrives. You want to go in?"

She nodded.

He slid from the SUV and came around to open her door. A gentleman. *Love it.* The front porch light flashed on and she flinched.

"Sorry," Brent said. "Motion sensor. Should have warned you."

"No problem."

Side by side, they walked to the porch. Brent swung his keys on his index finger once, twice, three times, and then snatched them into his hand.

Jenna stopped at the base of the stairs. "What about other suspects?"

"The sheriff thinks it might have been a robbery gone bad. Back then the only one in town who locked their door was my dad. Every night after he came home he'd lock up. My mom would wait for him. The working theory is an intruder came through the unlocked back door and tried to rob the place."

"Do you believe that?"

"Maybe. Carlisle isn't that big. Eight hundred people. Everyone knows everyone. There was a junkie who lived across town. He's moved away since, but they looked at him hard thinking he needed cash to score drugs. Couldn't make a case."

Junkie. Jenna made a note on the pad she'd brought from the car. "Does the sheriff know where he is?"

"I keep tabs on him. I'll get you his address. Then there's my dad. He left work that night and said he came straight home. No one knows what time he left the plant, and there was no security video inside the plant back then. He punched out at midnight, but theoretically his buddies could have punched him out. Guys did that all the time."

"How does that feel?"

"What?"

Please. Did he even realize how repressed his emotions were? At some point, Brent would need to stop burying the agony of his mother's death and let himself grieve. Obviously, now was not the time because this boy was locked up tight. "Thinking about your dad killing your mother. How does that feel?"

He climbed the stairs, waving her forward. "I have no idea."

"Pardon?"

Facing her, he let out a long breath and scrubbed his hand over his face. "I can't go there. I've thought about it over the years, but I don't want to believe he could do that to her."

"Did they argue a lot?"

He shrugged. "He yelled. She yelled back. Beyond that, I don't know. I was too young to draw any conclusions about whether they were happy or not."

And somehow, with all this trapped inside, he'd managed to stay sane.

"Anyway," he said. "The sheriff's name is Barnes. He's on board with you poking around, but don't irritate him. He needs to be involved."

She wrote the sheriff's name down so she could check him out. Maybe ask her dad's contacts about him. "Involved to what extent?"

If she had to check in before every move, they'd be sunk. She didn't and wouldn't work that way. Part of being good at her job—at least she hoped—meant shifting on the fly. She had no interest in checking in every ten minutes.

"To the extent where you don't aggravate or blindside him. If you're coming here, give him a heads-up. If you get a solid lead, give him a heads-up. If you want to question one of his citizens, give him a heads-up. Beyond that, I've got your back. You need a battle fought with him, I'm your guy. I know his buttons, and that makes me good at not pushing them."

And, oh, her heart went pitter-patter. This man, screwed-up emotions and all, might be her dream come true. He knew how to work people without them turning on him. "Brent Thompson, I think we'll make a great team." She faced the house, took in the peeling paint on the front door and breathed in. "Take me inside. We've got work to do."

Chapter Three

Brent shoved his key in the lock on the front door, stared down at the weathered handle and held his breath. Beside him, Jenna moved, ratcheting up his already spring-loaded tension. Straightening his shoulders, he released the breath he'd been holding.

"Are you okay?" Jenna asked, her voice mixing with the whistling wind.

With all the open space out here, he'd grown immune to the wind noise. Except tonight. Tonight that wind could have been a brass band in his head. Why tonight should be any different from the thousands of other times he'd stepped into this house, he wasn't clear on, but it definitely had something to do with Jenna-the-investigator, a near stranger wearing that red blouse with the extra unfastened button still taunting him, entering his space. The place where his life had been decimated.

"Brent?"

One, two, three. Go.

He turned the lock and shoved open the door. "I'm good. Just thinking." Flipping the inside light switch, he stepped over the threshold. "Come in."

When Jenna stepped in, he closed the door, shut out that damned wind and pointed to the living room floor. "Crime scene."

Jenna glanced around, taking in the sofa and the end tables all covered with sheets. Her gaze traveled to the front windows and the dusty drapes. Last time he'd been here, he'd forgotten to close them. Not a huge deal since his aunt and uncle watched over the place. Even if someone wanted to break in, what would they get? Thirty-year-old furniture. That's all. Everything else had been tossed or cleared out, all their childhood memories and valuables split between Brent and Camille.

All that was left here was the place his mother had died.

"Wow," Jenna finally said.

"Yeah."

"This is the original furniture?"

"Yes. The floor, too." He gestured to the hardwood. "It's never been refinished. In case you were wondering."

"I was. Thank you."

"Everything is relatively the same."

She took a step, and then halted before turning back to him. "May I?"

"Can't investigate standing here."

She walked around the furniture, peeled back a corner of a sheet to inspect the sofa then backed up to study the floor. After a minute, she squatted and ran her hand over the area where he'd found his mother beaten and bloody. Suddenly, the way Jenna's black slacks stretched over her rear seemed a whole lot better to think about.

Yeah, think about the beautiful woman instead. For once, he'd let his baser needs take the lead.

"Your bedroom is down this hallway?"

At that, he blurted a laugh. What timing.

"What's funny?"

He shook his head. "Nothing. Yes, bedroom is down the hall."

She inched closer to the sofa and his palms tingled, the flicking shooting straight up his arms into his chest.

"Right there," he said.

Jenna stopped and looked back at him. Her eyes, her body, the way she moved, all of it left him…*affected.*

"What?" she asked.

"One step to your right. That's where she was when I came down the hallway."

Without moving, she stared at the floor, studying the details—the grain of the wood, the seams where blood had seeped, the scuff marks—he'd spent years obsessing over.

Outside, a car door slammed. Sheriff Barnes arriving. Brent turned away from Jenna to open the door. The cruiser was parked behind his SUV. Brent held up a hand. "Hey, Sheriff."

Barnes, in the drab beige uniform the Carlisle Sheriff's Department had used since Brent could remember, strode to the porch, hat in place, bat belt—otherwise known as his gun belt—snug on his hips. Over the years, Barnes had filled out, but at nearly fifty-eight, he could still chase down perps.

He shook Brent's hand. "Brent, good to see you."

Not really, but what else was the guy supposed to say? "Thanks for coming, Sheriff. Come in."

Barnes stepped into the house, spotted the gorgeous brunette in the killer blouse and did a double take. *Right there with ya.* Every damned time Brent looked at her he had that same feeling. A little helpless, a little stunned and a whole lot horny.

Jenna glanced up, smiled and strutted toward them. Brent cleared his throat. "Sheriff Barnes, this is Jenna Hayward, the investigator I was telling you about."

Barnes shot him a look, and then shook his head. "But damn, if I had an investigator that looked like her, my crime rate would skyrocket. Everyone would want to be investigated."

In Brent's office, if he'd made a comment like that, his

superiors would have sent him to sensitivity training. Out here in Carlisle? No one much cared because they knew Barnes was a good, honest man who'd sooner sever his own hand than use it to touch a woman other than his wife. Unsure how Jenna would feel about the remark, he turned to her, offered an apologetic nod.

"Now, Sheriff," Jenna said, "you'd better watch yourself. I tend to get bored easily and may come looking for a job."

Barnes shook Jenna's extended hand, locked eyes with her, and the way she smiled, all crooked and *come-get-me*, once again reminded Brent how she used her looks to play men.

Particularly ones foolish enough to get played.

Finally, the sheriff got a hold of himself, straightened up and turned to Brent. "I have the copies you wanted in the car."

"Thank you." Brent swirled his finger. "I was about to review the scene with Jenna."

"Want me to do that?"

Not a bad idea, but he wanted to give his version of what he knew from that night. "I'll handle the first part and you can summarize the investigation. That work?"

"Whatever you're comfortable with."

"Sheriff," Jenna said, "I appreciate you letting me look at your files. A lot of people wouldn't."

Barnes shifted his hat between his hands. "I was a deputy back then and this was my first murder case."

His gaze went to the floor, the spot where Brent's mother had died, and the damned flicking stabbed up Brent's arms again. Anymore, he couldn't be in this house without the failure tearing at him. He inched his shoulders back and focused on Jenna.

"Anyway," Barnes said, "this case has stayed with me. I've got patience, but I need someone with imagination who can see more than I'm seeing. All I know is I want it solved."

Didn't they all.

Brent gestured down the hallway to his childhood bedroom where the hell began. "Let's start there."

JENNA FOLLOWED BRENT down the corridor, tracking his footsteps on the threadbare rug as he demonstrated the path that led him to discovering his mother's body. She glanced up at the peeling wallpaper—white with roses—and wondered how long it had been there.

"I looked out the door, but didn't see anything," Brent said. "My parents' bedroom door was closed, so I went to the living room, where the television was still on."

Something in his tone, the flatness, the lack of emotion, the *detachment*, again struck Jenna as odd. This was his mother and he was reciting these facts as if reading from a script.

"The house was quiet," he continued. "I figured my mom had fallen asleep on the couch. She did that sometimes."

Jenna jotted notes as she walked. At least until Brent stopped short and—*smash!*—she collided with him. Her chin bounced off his back, her pad fell to the floor and her pen…well…that sucker plunged into him. She gasped, dropped it and instinctively rubbed the wounded spot. A spot that happened to be on Brent Thompson's extremely tight backside.

The shock of her hand in a place it seriously shouldn't have been must have registered because he spun toward her.

Holy cow! She'd just groped a US marshal.

And liked it.

What a nightmare. She smacked her hand against her chest. *Bad, hand, bad.* A horrified giggle blurted out. *And it gets worse.*

"Okay," she said. "I'm going to beg you to believe that

was a completely—*completely*—unintentional thing. It was a reaction. If I'd hit your arm, I'd have grabbed it. I swear to you. Total accident."

Defuse it. Yes. That's what she'd do. Before they both started stuttering. She leaned forward, went on tiptoe and, keeping her voice low, she added, "But seriously, your back-side is a work of art. Pure heaven."

At that, Brent's lips spread slowly, like melting butter inching across his face, and Jenna's brain seized. The man had a smile—one he didn't show too often—that could spark a fire in a saturated forest.

"Heaven, huh?"

"Pure. I am sorry, though. Really."

Not really.

"You don't look sorry."

But the sinful grin told her he was enjoying the game as much as she was. Sure, she liked flirting. Did it often and with purpose. But with Brent, it was just plain fun. They both knew the spark was there. They'd just chosen not to do anything with it.

At least until she'd groped him and decided they definitely needed to do something with it.

The sheriff stepped into view at the end of the hallway. "It got quiet. You two okay?"

Brent's gaze traveled to the open buttons on her blouse and back up, giving her a heavy dose of eye contact. "Are we okay?"

"We are A-okay, Sheriff. Just having a little powwow here."

"Powwow," Brent said. "Is that what it's called?"

"It is now, big boy."

A squeak from the back of the house sounded and Brent winced, the move so small she'd almost missed it. In the second it took him to realize she'd witnessed his unguarded response, he threw his shoulders back and jerked a thumb toward the end of the hallway.

"Someone's at the back door. Probably my uncle. Let me check this."

Turning from her, he strode to the end of the hall, hung a right and headed to the kitchen.

If it was his uncle, she'd get an opportunity to put a face to a name. As she always did, she'd lay on the Miss Illinois-Runner-Up charm and let him get comfortable with her before interviewing him. She may have been rejected by the FBI, but they were clueless at how adept she was at handling men. Her four brothers could attest to that.

Regardless, everyone here the night of the murder needed to be interviewed. Any one of them could hold one small detail they deemed irrelevant, but might actually be important. Anything was possible.

Even twenty-three years later.

"Hey," Brent said. "Figured it was you."

"We just came from dinner." Male voice. A little gravelly. Older. "I saw your car outside. You didn't call."

Jenna and the sheriff stood in the living room giving Brent privacy with his uncle. At least she guessed it was his uncle.

"The day got away from me," Brent said. "Come into the living room. I want you to meet someone."

"Really?" The gravelly voice raised with that recognizable tone every unmarried, twenty-eight-year-old woman knew and sometimes, in her case, despised.

Did Brent's uncle think he was bringing a love interest home to meet his family? And what? Showing his girlfriend the place where his mother was murdered?

Twisted.

But, well, she'd seen plenty of *twisted* in this line of work. Simply put, people were weird. Brent just didn't strike her as one of the weird ones.

"Don't get ahead of yourself," Brent said.

"You're not getting any younger."

Finally, Brent laughed. "As you keep telling me."

He stepped into the room, his uncle on his heels. Given Brent's size it was no shocker that his uncle stood a good six inches shorter. He wore tattered jeans with an untucked flannel shirt over a T-shirt. His scuffed work boots clunked against the hardwood as he came into the room. Under the brim of his baseball cap, one which Jenna's mother would ask him to remove in the house, his gaze shot to Jenna and then to the sheriff.

He nodded. "Sheriff, everything all right?"

"Just fine, Herb. Brent asked me to meet him here."

"Uncle Herb, this is Jenna Hayward."

Herb removed his cap, came toward her and shook her hand. "Hello."

"Jenna is a private investigator."

That got his attention. He looked at Brent, and then swung back to Jenna.

"No fooling?"

"No fooling," she said. "I work for a law firm."

Brent waggled a hand. "Remember the lawyer from last spring?"

"The mouthy blonde?"

"Seriously," Brent said, "you did not just say that."

Oh, he sure had and Jenna couldn't help smiling at the spot-on description of her boss. "That's her. She's one of my bosses."

Brent glanced at her. "Sorry. They were asking me about Penny and I was trying to describe her. I didn't mean it the way it sounds." He went back to his uncle. "Jenna is helping on Mom's case. The sheriff came by with files."

"Good to hear. I'm glad you'll get some help on this." Brent's uncle addressed Jenna. "We need to get her justice. She was a good girl."

His uncle gripped Brent's arm, clearly a gesture of affection and support, and something kicked against Jenna's ribs. Brent's father may have abandoned his family, but his uncle sure hadn't. These poor people. All these years they'd been struggling with loss and heartbreak and injustice. "Brent, do you mind if I talk with your uncle a bit?"

He shrugged. "Sure."

But Brent didn't move.

"Alone?"

For a moment, he continued to stand there and then he blinked. *There we go.* Slowly, it all registered. "Gotcha. I'll walk outside with the sheriff. Get those files for you."

"And, hey," his uncle said, "head over and see your aunt. She misses you. Jamie is there. Catch her before she goes home."

Jamie. Brent's cousin. He'd mentioned her on the ride over.

On his way out, Brent waved in that yeah-yeah-yeah way people used when being nagged. The front door closed and Jenna moved next to Herb. He focused on her face, which she'd give him bonus points for. "Thanks again for helping," Brent's uncle said.

"No need to thank me. Brent is a good guy. I had no idea about his mom. It's…well…tragic."

"It is. But Brent, he turned out to be a damned fine man. Taking care of his sister the way he did. A lot of boys would run from that. Not him. He latches on."

He sure did. "So it seems. May I ask you some questions regarding the night his mom died?"

"Whatever you need. But the sheriff has it all in his notes."

Of course he did, but hearing it *and* reading it were necessities. "Yes, but since we're here, I was hoping you could walk me through what went on when you got here."

He took in the room, studying the now-uncovered furniture. His gaze landed on the floor in front of the sofa. Slowly, he ran his hand over his face, a gesture so similar to the one she'd seen Brent use it sent a chill up her arms. Like father like son, only this wasn't the father and Brent wasn't the son.

Finally, he looked back at Jenna. "She was a mess. Poor thing. I found her right here. Right where I'm standing."

The exact spot Brent had indicated. "When did you first see Brent?"

"He came to the house, ran inside—we never locked the doors back then—screaming and crying. Scared the hell out of me." He shook his head. "Long as I live, I'll never get the sound of that boy's screams out of my system."

It was hard to picture. Strong, solid Brent at five, terrified and begging for help. She hated the thought. Hated the idea that he'd dealt with that trauma. "What time was this?"

"Just after midnight. Maybe 12:10."

After checking her notes and confirming the time with what Brent told her, she pointed at the front door. "You came in this way?"

"Yes, ma'am. Usually we come in the back. Cheryl always kept that door unlocked. That night, Brent must have run out the front door because it was open when I got here."

"Brent was with you?"

That might have been a trick question—no might about it—because she knew where Brent had been. He'd told her. Still, it never hurt to let the witness give his own assessment.

"No. He was back at the house. Poor kid was howling something about his mom and blood. My wife called 9-1-1 and I came back to check on Cheryl and get the baby—Brent's sister. We always call her the baby."

Staying focused on the scene, Jenna moved to the entryway. "So you're on the porch and the door is open."

"Yeah." He walked over and opened the door, letting a

burst of cool air in as he pushed it back against the wall. "It was like this when I came in."

Jenna faced the living room, accessing the layout—sofa blocking her view of where the body would have been, the end table and side chair that could have hindered the murderer—all of it part of an investigation that had gone nowhere in twenty-three years.

Herb walked back to the sofa and pointed. "She was right there. Kind of curled up, but not really. Her hair was all bloody."

Head wounds bled more than others due to all the blood vessels. Jenna had learned that from her dad.

She drew a map of the room, marking an X where the body had been found. "Were these chairs here back then?"

"Yes. They may have moved them when they were living here, but Brent put everything back when he started working on the case."

"Then what happened?"

Herb scratched his cheek and then gestured to the floor. "I leaned over her, checked her pulse. I couldn't find one, but I'm no doctor. By then, Barnes—he was a deputy then—had pulled in. I ran back to get Camille before she woke up."

More notes. He'd left the body so he could get Camille. Parental instinct would be to protect the child. Made sense. "The sheriff arrived and you went back to your house with Camille? Did she see the body?"

"No. I covered her eyes when I carried her out. I took her next door and came back. My wife was trying to get hold of Mason."

"Brent's father?"

"Yes, ma'am. She wanted to warn him, but we didn't have cell phones back then, and he'd already left work. I waited for him to pull up while the paramedics were in here with Cheryl." He flipped his palms up, and then let them drop. "Helluva night, that one."

The heaviness in his voice, weight saddling his vocal chords, drew her gaze. For her, this was a job. For them, she couldn't imagine. "Do you need a break?"

"Maybe I do." He started for the door, but then stopped and gestured to the floor. "All these years I've been thinking about what my nephew saw. I don't know how a boy recovers from that."

Jenna's guess was the boy in question hadn't recovered. All he'd done was bury the pain deep enough that it would allow him to go forward, to keep searching, to get justice.

Only problem was, all the anger he'd stuffed inside him would eventually go boom. And that would cause an emotional landslide.

Obviously wanting to be done, Herb turned toward the still open door. "Do you need anything else?"

"Not right now. I'm sorry if I upset you."

"It's all right. I want to help. If we solve this, it'll give Brent and Camille peace. Maybe then he'll sell this damned house."

"It must be hard living right next door."

He shrugged. "If someone lived here, gave the house some life, it wouldn't be so bad. Now it's just an empty place where my sister-in-law died. It's a damned morgue."

OUTSIDE, THE GARAGE spotlight illuminated the driveway, and Brent spotted his aunt Sylvie marching across the patch of grass separating the two homes. She made a direct line for him, her face, as usual, passive. No pinched brows, no big smile, no tight cheeks. Nothing to indicate her mood. He'd always said she'd make a great spy. Bringing up the rear was his cousin, Jamie, who wore that slightly amused grin that meant she wasn't the only one in trouble.

He shifted his gaze back to his aunt and—yep—all that passive behavior meant one thing, she was about to yell at him for staying away so long.

Might as well take it like a man.

While the sheriff unloaded the copies of evidence files, Brent walked across the driveway, the heels of his dress shoes clapping against the pavement and the lack of traffic noise reminded him that he wasn't in Chicago anymore. Coming back here, with all the contrasts to the city, brought back all that bubbling agony he fought to control. And he didn't want that. He wanted it buried where he didn't have to deal with it. What he needed was to stay strong—for Camille, for his aunt and for his uncle.

They could turn into basket cases if they chose, but not him. His day would come, though. When they found his mother's killer, then he'd figure out how to deal with all the garbage he'd packed inside him.

"Hey, Aunt Sylvie." He held out his arms and his much smaller aunt stepped into them.

"Don't *Hey-Aunt-Sylvie* me, young man. You know you're in trouble. You didn't even call to tell us."

She backed away from the hug and stared up at him. Since his mother had died, his aunt had turned her fanatical focus on him and Camille. Whether it was her own grief or simply wanting to make sure they had a mother figure in their lives—maybe both—was still up for debate, but Brent never questioned it. Aunt Sylvie always made sure they were cared for and had hot food in their bellies.

For that reason alone, he always answered when she called. No matter what.

Even when she griped at him.

"I know. I'm sorry. I got caught up at work and didn't get a chance to call."

Jamie stepped around her mother, went on tiptoes and smacked a kiss on Brent's cheek. "Hey, cuz. Good to see you."

"Hi, James."

He'd started calling his cousin James when they were

kids and the nickname had stuck. She never seemed to mind.

Obviously done ranting, Aunt Sylvie waved at Barnes, who'd finished digging a file box from his car and had set it on the trunk. "Sheriff, how are you?"

"I'm good, Sylvie. You all right?"

"Oh, we're just fine." She shot Brent the stink-eye. "Wouldn't mind seeing my niece and nephew a little more."

Guilt, Brent had enough of. Hell, he had enough guilt to fill the Chicago River. "You know how to drive. And Chicago is only an hour."

As usual, her mouth dropped open and she gasped. "Look at you with that smart mouth."

"Merely an observation."

Jamie cleared her throat. "What's in the box, Sheriff?"

The sheriff glanced at Brent, unsure how much to reveal, so Brent took that one. "That's for me. Copies of Mom's files."

With that bright spotlight shining down on her, Aunt Sylvie whipped her gaze between Brent and the sheriff. Brent knew right where her mind had gone. "Has something happened? A lead?"

Dang. He'd been insensitive. He knew her. Knew how her mind worked and the slow-curling panic that fired every time the sheriff pulled into one of these driveways.

And Brent hadn't warned her.

Gave her zero notice about Jenna investigating. *Moron.*

Brent touched her arm. "No. But there's someone I'll introduce you to in a minute. She's inside talking with Uncle Herb. I think she can help us."

"Who is she?"

"An investigator. Remember the lawyer I helped last spring?"

"That adorable little blonde?"

Adorable. Penny would hate that. She'd like Uncle Herb's description better. "Yes. The investigator works for her law firm. They offered to help with Mom's case."

Aunt Sylvie cocked her head. "She's good, this investigator?"

"She is."

And she's got a body that drives me insane. Not that he'd say that, but he was a man, and men had needs. Needs that Brent had been sorely neglecting lately. Needs that maybe Jenna could help him with.

When they were done finding a killer.

Because as much as Brent fantasized about a long night with Jenna in his bed, his priority was catching his mother's killer. If he and Jenna got involved, something told him it would get ugly when he walked away. And walk away, he would. He liked coming and going as he pleased and not having to explain himself to anyone. He didn't see that changing anytime soon.

The snick of the front-door latch sounded and they all turned toward the house. Jenna came down the porch steps.

She walked toward them, her coat flying open to reveal her blouse and the slacks that fit her curvy body in all the right ways.

"Wow," Jamie said. "She's pretty."

Aunt Sylvie gave him a bored look. "*This* is your investigator?"

Brent grinned. "Yep!"

"Which body part made this decision?" she whispered.

"Well, look at you with that smart mouth," he said in his best Sylvie voice.

Without giving her an opportunity to respond, he waved Jenna over. "Come meet my aunt and cousin."

After doing the introductions, Brent turned to Aunt Sylvie. "Jenna will be poking around. Don't freak when you see a car in the driveway."

"Yes," Jenna said. "I'd like to chat with both of you, at your convenience, of course."

Aunt Sylvie pressed her lips together, and then shot a look at Uncle Herb who nodded. She didn't like talking about her sister. Ever. Growing up, Brent had craved stories about his mom, but the memories were too painful for his aunt and she typically ran from the room sobbing. Over the years, Brent had been conditioned not to talk about his mother. Which pretty much stunk.

"Of course," his aunt said. "If it'll help. I'm available anytime."

"Thank you. I'd like to read through the sheriff's files first. Would it be all right if I call you in a day or two?" She looked at Jamie. "Both of you?"

"Sure," Jamie said. "Anytime."

"Thank you."

"Well, have you eaten?" his aunt asked Brent. "I could fix you something."

A meal would serve him good right now, but the night had dragged on and, as hopeful as he was about the new energy Jenna brought, talking about his mother, reliving that night, had drained him. Time to get back to Chicago, where the sounds of the city would drown the noise in his head. Silence, he'd learned long ago, was his enemy. During high school and college, football helped smother it. With football, the energy it took to step to the line and get his head beat in was all the distraction he needed. When he became a marshal—nothing boring there—silence was no longer an issue. Pretty much, the US Marshal Service was involved in everything from judicial and witness security to asset forfeiture. If it involved federal laws, US marshals were there. One day he could chase down a fugitive, the

next make sure a witness didn't get blown away by someone they'd just testified against.

Out here, in his childhood hometown where the streets
were desolate after six o'clock and the only outside noise
came from birds or cicadas or blowing leaves, the quiet
created emotional chaos.

Gotta go.

He leaned down, kissed his aunt's cheek. "We need to
get back to the city. Maybe on the weekend."

"Saturday," she said. "After church."

He laughed. By now he should know better than to throw
out a maybe. His aunt took a maybe and turned it into a
definitely.

"You could come early and go to church with us."

Now she wanted church too. Years since he'd done that.
Which was a shame. He used to enjoy church, but now it
gave him too much time to reflect on things he shouldn't
reflect on. "Don't push it. Saturday for dinner. I'll be here.
I'll see what Camille is doing. Don't worry. I'll channel
the guilt from you."

She waved her hands. "Oh, with the sass."

He kissed her again. "I love you. Good night."

"I love you, too. Drive carefully. No speeding."

"Yes, ma'am."

He turned to Jenna. "All set?"

Please let her be all set.

She nodded. "You bet."

He shook hands with the sheriff. "Thank you. I'll call
you with any updates."

"I'd appreciate that."

On the way to his SUV, he grabbed the file box off the
back of the sheriff's cruiser, the weight of it, as always,
easy to handle. Most of what was in that file he'd probably
seen already. Except for the photos. Being a marshal, he'd
learned to take emotion out of a case. Even when it came

to his mother. He could read the forensics reports, investigator notes and the autopsy report. All of it, he could handle. Even some of the crime scene photos showing the exterior of the house or certain pieces of evidence were tolerable. But not the ones of his mom's body. Those were a different damned beast, and he couldn't find a compartment big enough to control the massive anger those pictures would unleash.

Balancing the box against the SUV, he opened the back door, shoved the box on the seat and walked around to get Jenna's door. By the time he'd gotten there, she already had her hand on the handle.

"I've got it," he said.

"Again with this?"

When he'd picked her up at her apartment, she'd teased him about the gesture. What she didn't know was his aunt would skin him if he abandoned his manners. Plus, he liked doing it. "Yeah. Again with this. Get used to it and don't argue."

He held open the door and waved her into the car. To that, she tilted her chin up and saluted. "Yes, sir."

And the look on her face, so serious with her cheeks sucked in and her gaze straight ahead, made him laugh. Really laugh.

In front of his mother's house no less. Helluva thing.

She slid into the car and the interior light illuminated her face and the grin that—*wait for it*—would cause the punch to his chest. Jenna Hayward was beautiful, but she wasn't one of those everyday beautiful women you could find anywhere you looked. On sight, she took a man's legs out from under him. *Bam!*

He leaned in to get a whiff of her perfume, something floral but light. Not allergy inducing. *Thank you*. Once again, his eyes went to that extra undone button on her blouse and the lush skin under it. He caught a glimpse of lace and swore under his breath. "Okay, Miss Illinois, cut the wisecracks."

She straightened up. "Miss Illinois?"

"You think I'm going to let you anywhere near my mother's case without checking you out?"

HE KNEW. Not that it was some big secret, but she didn't necessarily flaunt her beauty queen background. In her line of work, it didn't gain her anything. All she knew was that at the age of twenty-one, after years of working the pageant circuit, years of hearing her mother coo over how beautiful her daughter was, and the resulting pressure of it all, she'd had enough. Enough of the dieting, enough of having to look a certain way at all times, enough of the show. She simply wanted to be Jenna. A pretty girl who liked to eat cake and pester her detective father with questions about cases.

Playing along, she scissored Brent's silky tie between two fingers. Nice tie. Nice man. Nice everything. And she so adored the way he interacted with his family. Teasing, but firm and loving when they tried to give him any nonsense.

"My pageant days aren't classified information. All you have to do is check Google. And, by the way, you failed. I didn't win. I was the runner-up."

His lips lifted slightly as he watched her play with his tie. "I didn't fail. I knew that, but decided it wasn't worth mentioning. Those judges were either blind or stupid. I'm guessing beauty contest judges need eyesight, so that leaves stupid."

Did that just send a hot flash raging? This was their problem. That connection, that heat she couldn't ignore. "Marshal Thompson, are you flirting with me?"

"Nope. Calling it like I see it."

She flicked away the tie. "I was fifteen pounds lighter then."

Where did that come from? Sure, her brothers liked to taunt her about packing on a few pounds, but her pageant weight was impossible to maintain. And Jenna had a thing for food. In that she liked it.

"Yet another tragedy," Brent said.

"What?"

"That you were fifteen pounds lighter."

In the lit interior of the car, she studied his face. Looking for the tell that he was charming her into possibly removing her clothes. Which, if he kept talking like that, just might happen. Without a doubt, every one of her brain cells must have evaporated. Only explanation for this attack of flightiness.

"You don't like skinny women?"

"Brent?" his aunt called from the front of the house. "Everything okay?"

He backed away and straightened. "We're good! Seat belt jammed."

He shut the door, came around the driver's side, hopped in and fired the engine. "If we stay here, she'll be all over us."

Jenna waited. Would he answer her about the skinny women thing? Part of her wanted to know. The other part wanted to run. Although the extra fifteen pounds had only brought her to a size eight, it still bothered her. Made her wonder what men saw when they looked at the ex-beauty queen whose body had gone fluffy.

At the road, Brent hit the gas and the car tore through the blackness of the country road, the only sound being the radio on low volume. Tim McGraw maybe, but Jenna couldn't tell. She was more of a pop music girl.

"No," Brent said.

"No what?"

"I don't like skinny women. And it's a damned shame you think you looked better fifteen pounds lighter because, honey, you're wrong."

Oh, she might like where this conversation was heading. "I don't think I looked better."

"Liar."

"Hey!"

"Just admit it and be done with it. I saw your picture—nice gown by the way—and I can promise you, from a completely male perspective, you looked like a bean pole back then. A guy my size would break that girl in half."

"Did you somehow get drunk when you were outside with your family?"

He smiled at that and she liked the sight of it.

"Calling it like I see it," he said again.

"Well, thank you, I suppose. For the compliment."

"You're welcome."

"It never hurts to hear someone appreciates your looks."

For a quick second, he turned and the dashboard glow lit his face as he helped himself to a look at her body. "I definitely appreciate your looks. I'd imagine most men do. I think you know that."

The side of his mouth quirked again—all male and sexy and devilish—and my, oh, my, Jenna's stomach did a flip. "You're flirting with me."

"I might be."

"Is that wise?"

He laughed. "Probably not. But as I recall, you do your share of flirting."

She shifted sideways in her seat and the belt scraped the side of her neck. Darn it, that'd leave a mark. Forget it. She needed a snappy comeback, but the big ox was right. Her flirting wasn't personal, though. *What?* How insane would she sound if she said that? When she flirted, she did it to get somewhere, to make progress. Flirting for her had become a tactic. A strategic tool in her arsenal.

"We're adults," she said. "Let's just throw it out there that there's chemistry between us. Or am I totally wrong?"

Sounding a little desperate here, Jenna. What was it with her? Always needing the ego boost. Always needing approval. Blame it on her years of being judged in contests and her failure to get into the FBI, but she couldn't get through the day without wondering what people thought of her.

"You're not wrong."

"About the chemistry, or flirting not being wise?"

"Both."

She sighed, turned to the front again. "I need to do a good job on this, Brent. It's important to me."

"News flash, honey, it's important to me, too. If you don't want me flirting with you, I won't flirt, but you set that tone the second I met you in the hallway outside Penny's office last spring. Make up your mind what you want from me, Jenna. If you want this all business, it'll be all business. It can't be both ways. You decide."

This man could have grown up in her household. So direct and strong and honest. "I want to do a good job for you. For your mom. She deserves that."

"Yes, she does."

"I like flirting with you. For once, it's not a prop. It's fun and you have a great smile that I don't think you show enough. It makes me feel good that I can get you to smile."

And again, it all rolled around to what made her feel good. Pathetic. She waved her hands and looked out the window. "No flirting."

"Fine. No flirting. And yeah, you get me to smile, and that doesn't happen a lot."

So much for no flirting.

"There's one thing I want to know."

"What's that?"

He glanced at her. "I'm not being a jerk here, I'm seriously curious."

"I've been warned. Ask away."

"How does someone go from being the runner-up in the Miss Illinois pageant to being a private investigator? And, again, I'm not being a jerk."

"I don't mind. People have asked me this question a million times. My father is a career detective. I've always been fascinated by what he does. I'd sit and ask him questions. Two of my four brothers are also cops and will probably make detective. I guess you could say we played a lot of real-life *Clue* when I was little."

"So, how'd you get to being a PI? Why not join the PD?"

Leave it to him to pursue it. Most people were satisfied with the my-dad-is-a-detective line and dropped the subject. Not Brent. He had to know it all. She looked out the window where the tollway lights dimmed in the distance.

She turned back to him. "I was a psychology major in college."

"I could see that. You study people."

"I like to know what makes them tick. After I graduated, I couldn't see myself in an office all day counseling people. I needed to be out and moving, so I applied for the FBI."

He shot her a look, and then went back to the road. "You wanted to be an agent?"

"I did. And I wanted it bad."

"Did you go to the academy?"

"Nope. Never made it that far. They rejected me."

There, she'd said it. Not many people knew and she held her breath, waited for a crack about the beauty queen wanting to play G-man, or in her case, G-woman.

But Brent watched the road ahead as the tollway entrance drew closer. *Shouldn't have said anything.* The man was a US marshal. He'd succeeded where she'd failed. What did she expect him to say? *Dumb, Jenna.* Heat rose in her cheeks—thank goodness the car was dark—and she rested her head back.

"That's a shame," he said. "You'd have made a good agent. You wouldn't have needed your cleavage to do it, either. Don't sell yourself short, Jenna. You're beautiful, but you're smart, too. Don't ever forget that."

The air in her chest stalled and she squeezed her eyes closed. No one, not even her mother who often rolled her eyes at Jenna's clothing choices, had ever said that. *He knew.* But she couldn't get crazy here. He wasn't offering a glass slipper. All he offered was an opinion.

Still resting her head back, she eased out a breath. "You might be flirting with me, but I don't care. Thank you for saying that."

He shrugged. "That time I wasn't flirting. It's not complicated. I like you and you've got a brain. You don't need to be half-naked to be good at what you do."

Suddenly, Jenna wished he'd been flirting, because she might have just fallen a little in love with Brent Thompson.

Chapter Four

Two days later, on a sunlit Saturday morning that reminded Jenna that October could be a beautiful month, she pulled into the driveway of Brent's childhood home and absorbed her first daytime sight of it. What she'd missed the other night was the peeling paint on the porch poles, the rotting window frames and the roof that needed to be replaced. All of it added to the permeating sadness from a house that hadn't been truly lived in—or loved—for years.

And here she was, digging up—metaphorically—the body buried there. After sorting through the copies of reports, photos and witness statements the sheriff had provided, Jenna needed more time at the scene. Something bugged her. And the lack of a murder weapon was top on her list.

Blunt force trauma. That's all the report had said. Crime scene photos showed a wound with a right angle. Square weapon? Possibly, but that could be anything. A trophy, a kitchen appliance, a statue. Plenty of household items had square bottoms.

Across the yard, Brent's cousin exited her parents' home. Like the other night, Jamie wore her shoulder-length dark blond hair pushed back in a headband that Jenna assumed was her go-to look. Also her go-to look would be loose jeans and a navy sweatshirt on her average-sized frame, and

Jenna found herself a little envious of the comfort wear. The only place Jenna wore that look was inside her own home.

Jamie spotted the strange car in the driveway and paused. Finally, recognition dawned and Jamie waved.

Time to work.

Jenna gathered her purse and her briefcase and swung open the car door. A crisp breeze blew her hair sideways and she shoved it from her face. Next time, she'd do a ponytail. With all this open space, her hair couldn't be counted on to cooperate. "Hi, Jamie. How are you?"

"Hi. It's Jenna, right?"

"Sure is."

"No Brent?"

"He had errands this morning. He said he'd catch up with me in a bit."

Jamie turned toward the house, her gaze focused as her shoulders drooped. "He thinks he can handle all this, but I worry about him. This house is an albatross."

Negative energy oozed around Jenna, sending prickles up her arms. How did Brent's family stand the constant reminder of tragedy? Jamie shifted back to her, the fine lines around the woman's eyes deepening as she squinted. Being a woman who could peg another woman's age fairly accurately—a gift really—Jenna put Jamie at thirty-nine.

"You were a teenager when his mom died, right?"

"Yes. Fifteen."

Ooh, so close. Only a year off. "It must have been rough on all of you."

"Not as rough as Brent and Camille had it. And even my useless uncle."

Jenna nodded. "Brent told me about that. He said his father has always been a suspect."

"As far as I know."

"What do you think?"

"I think he's spineless and doesn't have the stomach for

murder. But I've lived in this town all my life and wouldn't have believed it would happen here, so what do I know?"

That was about as direct of an answer as Jenna could ask for. "Do your parents hear from Brent's father?"

"If they do, they don't tell me." She shrugged. "We don't talk about him much."

In an odd way, Jenna understood. Nothing would change the man abandoning his family, so what was the point of stewing? Stewing wasted time and already battered emotional reserves.

"Do you remember anything from that night?"

Jamie sighed. "Sometimes it feels like it was yesterday. I woke up when I heard the sirens. I came out of my room and my mom told me Brent and Camille were sleeping and I should be quiet. Then she sent me back to my room." Jamie turned, pointed to one of the side windows on her parents' house. "I watched from that window. I wasn't sure what happened, but I got scared—really scared— when I saw the ambulance. It was…"

She stopped, put one hand over her mouth and the other over her eyes. Her shoulders hitched and instant guilt landed on Jenna. She touched Jamie's arm. "I'm so sorry to put you through this."

After a few seconds, Jamie dropped her hands and heaved a giant breath. "It's not your fault. I know we have to do this."

"Thank you."

"Anyway, I saw Brent's dad arrive, and he started yelling and going crazy. I knew it had to be Aunt Cheryl."

The window Jamie had pointed to was midway between the front and rear of Brent's house, so Jenna walked to it and surveyed the immediate area. Only a sliver of the back porch could be seen from that location. "Did you see anyone come out the back? Maybe walk through here?"

"No. I was asleep until I heard the sirens."

Nothing here. And Jenna was losing precious time to restage the murder scene before Brent arrived. Based on witness statements found in the sheriff's file, she'd prepared a timeline showing when each person came into play. Who knew if it would amount to anything, but that was part of the investigative allure. Sometimes the most obscure details broke open a case.

Jenna wanted to break open this case.

Without asking, as she'd often done, for her father's advice. If it came down to it, she'd ask. Her ego wasn't so giant that she wouldn't seek help when needed, but for now she'd do this alone.

She walked back to Jamie. "Thank you for talking with me. Every little bit helps. I'm going to head inside and look around."

"Sure. I only came by to drop the pies off for tonight. My parents are out. Will you be all right by yourself?"

Jenna waved her off. God knew she'd been in worse places than this. Three weeks ago she'd been traipsing the south side of Chicago at two in the morning looking for a drug dealer, but she hadn't exactly been alone then. Like today, her .38 had accompanied her.

"I'll be fine. Brent will be along soon."

Jamie took a pen and scrap of paper from her purse. "Here's my cell number. I only live five minutes away. Call if you need anything."

"Thank you. I appreciate that."

"Anything I can do, just let me know."

Jenna stuck the paper in her jacket pocket and waited for Jamie to drive off before digging out the house key Brent had given her.

For a few minutes, she'd been afraid Jamie would stay and, at this stage, Jenna needed time alone at the scene. Family members would distract her. They'd stand around, disrupting the energy and asking questions when she needed quiet. If they didn't ask questions, they'd be thinking them and she'd sense it.

Times like these, it was better for her to work solo.

Inside, she dumped her purse on the floor and, remembering her father's constant warnings, locked the door behind her. Could never be too cautious. A spear of light through the closed drapes illuminated the darkened room. Jenna assumed someone must have closed the drapes after they'd left the other night. She flipped the light switch and the overhead fixture came on. Not great lighting, but it would do. And she had a flashlight if necessary.

She glanced around at the covered furniture. *Need to see it.* Yes. She'd pull off all the coverings to see what was under them, and then pull the cushions to search for bloodstains. Crime scene reports indicated blood had only been found on the floor, but Brent wanted fresh eyes and she would provide them.

She worked her way around the room, gently lifting sheets off the furniture. Even with minimal movements, dust particles floated.

Prickles snaked up her arms again. Sad existence, this house.

Unlike the exterior of the home, the dark blue upholstered side chairs were in good shape. No tears and minimal fading. In the crime scene photos the sofa was a floral pattern. One way to check. She spun back to the sofa and peeled the sheet off one arm. Underneath she found white fabric layered with different shades of red flowers.

She uncovered the rest of the sofa, still positioned in the spot where Brent's mother had died. Jenna would outline where the body had been found, go through her timeline and see if anything struck her. From her briefcase, she grabbed the crime scene photos and set them on the floor. Rather than put tape on the floor, she opted for string. Plus, if Brent walked in she could yank the string up quickly. As much as he played tough guy, she didn't want him to face an outline of his mother's body.

After measuring the distance from the windows and finding the exact location where the body had been, Jenna used the photos as a guide and positioned the string on the floor. From there she went to the back door and unlocked it. *Sorry, Dad. Have to do it.* The door had been unlocked the night of the murder and, for timeline purposes, Jenna needed everything as close to that night as possible.

"Door set. Body there. Murder weapon?"

She breathed in and her temples throbbed. *What the heck?* She wrapped her fingers around her forehead and squeezed. The crazy headache had come from nowhere. Or perhaps she'd been distracted. Either way, she had ibu-profen in her purse.

Along with her flashlight.

Flashlight. With no murder weapon she'd have to im-provise. She checked her watch. 12:30 p.m. *Darn it.* She'd been here forty-five minutes already and had spent too much time on the photos. *Dumb, Jenna.* Brent said he'd arrive by 1:00 p.m. and now she'd have to rush.

She hustled back to her purse and grabbed the flashlight-slash-improvised-murder weapon.

A snick sounded just on the other side of the door and she stood half frozen, flashlight in hand as the door came open. Brent's head snapped back and, all at once, his arms were in motion, reaching for his waist.

Gun. Blood barreled into her already aching head. *No, no, no.* "It's me!"

For three long seconds he stared at her, unblinking, his gaze hard and steady, but at least he wasn't reaching for his gun anymore.

"It's me," she repeated, her body losing some of the paralyzing tension.

Bending at the waist, he dropped his hands to his knees and shook his head. "You scared the hell out of me!"

"I…I…I'm sorry. I was getting something from my purse and heard the lock. You saw my car outside."

A gust of wind smacked the door against the interior wall and Brent stepped in, nudging her sideways so he could close it. "I know, but…" He scrubbed a hand over his face, shook his head.

"But what? You were about to draw on me."

He winced, then leaned back against the wall. "I'm sorry. Being here gets me crazy. All I saw was someone holding a weapon."

The flashlight. He'd thought it was a weapon. Ironic since she'd planned on using it as such for her reenactment. "Then I guess we scared each other."

"Hell, yeah. I'm not used to seeing someone on the other side of that door. Damned near gave me a heart attack."

He glanced around, spotted the sheets off and the photos scattered around. He turned his back to the room. "What are you doing?"

"I was, um, reviewing photos." She rushed to the photos and the body outline. "Hang there a second. Let me scoop this stuff up."

"It's okay. I'll…wait…what's that smell? Did you spray something?"

Did she *spray* something? "No."

He looked around, took in the room, the drapes, the furniture and then stared up at the ceiling. In a burst, he lunged back to the door quicker than a man his size should be able to move. He whipped open the door. "Out!"

What the heck? "Why?"

"Gas. Get out." He clamped on to her arm and dragged her to the door. "Didn't you smell the gas when you came in?"

"No. But I've been here awhile. I was distracted."

But the gas might be the reason for her sudden headache. Of course. What an idiot. Who doesn't smell gas?

Just as they got to the door, her foot wobbled on her skinny boot heel and her ankle gave way. Pain shot clear up to her knee, and she grabbed a fistful of Brent's jacket for balance. "Ow!"

"Are you passing out?"

Passing out? "No, dopey. I twisted my ankle."

"Don't call me dopey."

Suddenly, she went airborne and landed on Brent's shoulder in a *whoosh*. "What are you doing?"

"You just said you twisted your ankle. I'm getting us out. Or would you rather fry when the house blows from that gas leak? Your choice, Miss Illinois. I can take you back in."

Jenna gasped. What. A. Jerk. "Be nice."

"Hey, you called me dopey."

Brent marched down the stairs, moving quickly from the house. Apparently her weight wasn't an issue for this big boy. "I didn't mean it *that* way. I was teasing. Put me down."

"Which ankle hurts?"

"The left."

"When I put you down, don't put any pressure on it. Just lean back against your car."

With one hand on her back, he eased her to the ground. His hand slid over the side of her hip to her thigh where he held her leg. And, oh, the feel of his hand running down her body made that headache seem a whole lot less annoying. She lifted her foot, hung on to Brent's arm and levered onto the hood of her car.

"You good for a sec?" he asked. "I need to shut the gas off."

"I'm fine. Go."

He tore around the far side of the house, disappearing while she checked out her ankle. She set her foot down, didn't feel agonizing pain and considered it a bonus. So far, so good. She tried a little weight on it. Ew. A pang bolted up her calf, but nothing unbearable. "Junior ow."

If it were broken, she'd know. She hoped. Having never broken a foot or ankle, she wasn't sure. At the very least, she wouldn't be able to put weight on it, which she could do. If it was a sprain, she'd at least get around on it. Just not in high-heeled boots.

"What are you doing?" Brent shouted as he came around the side of the house, his face all hard and yummy angles.

Had to love a man on a mission. "I have sneakers in the car. I'm taking my boot off so I can put them on."

"Just stay in your sock. There's a doc in town. We can run over there and get it x-rayed." He squatted in front of her, pushed her hands away and lifted her foot. "I'll take the boot off. You ready?"

"It's not that bad. What's up with the gas?"

One hand braced around her calf, he guided the boot off and—wow—his touch was soft but with rough skin that caused friction. Friction and thoughts of Brent. Without clothes. All those solid muscles waiting for her to run her hands over. Jenna tilted her head up to the perfection of blue sky and prayed she didn't make a fool of herself in the next five seconds.

"I don't know," he said. "I turned the main off. I'll call the gas company and get them out here."

Needing to demolish the lust filling her body, she shooed him away. "Make the call. I'm fine."

"We're still getting it x-rayed after I make this call."

He dug into the front pocket of his jeans for his phone and dialed. While he waited for the operator to connect him, he scooted next to her, leaned against the car and patted his lap. "Slide that foot up here."

"Look at you being all Mr. Caretaker. I like it."

He shrugged. "Can't help it. I'm on hold. Let's hope the house doesn't blow."

"You left the front door open. It'll air out."

"True. Did you get anything done before I got here?"

Meaning, had she made any miraculous discoveries. Not yet. "I had everything set up and was about to run through my timeline when you showed up. I got waylaid by your cousin."

"She was here?"

Jenna nodded. "Dropping something off for your aunt. I got to talk to her a little bit about that night. She was watching from her window."

"I know. I read it in the file."

"Have the two of you ever talked about it?"

He waggled his free hand. "Some. I had questions related to the investigation and she answered them. That's about it."

Again with burying his emotions. How the hell did these people not discuss this? With her family, they talked about everything. Even her father. Maybe he wasn't free-wheeling with his emotions, but if something bothered him, he spoke up. Brent's family? Forget it? They were cinched so tight they'd never be free.

Jenna sighed. "That seems to be a habit with you."

BRENT'S BODY DAMNED near turned to stone. What the hell was Jenna muttering about? "What does *that* mean?"

Jenna eased her foot off his lap. Obviously the woman wasn't stupid and had a fine sense of when she'd irritated someone. Good for her because she'd just royally peeved him. He stood and shook out his legs while waiting for the gas company to take his *emergency* call.

"Brent, I don't think it's a shock to you that you hide your feelings about your mother. It's obviously a defense mechanism—self-preservation maybe. I don't blame you. I'm not sure I'd be able to do what you do without squashing all those feelings. Still, it's not healthy."

Unstable territory. And really, he didn't want to have

this conversation. Outside of discussing her case, he didn't talk about his mother. Or his feelings about her death. Why give rage room to drown him?

"I don't like to talk about her."

"I realize that."

Tired of the crummy hold music, he pulled the phone from his ear, put it on speaker and set it on the hood of her car. "Then why are you bugging me about it?"

"I'm not. I made an observation. It's what I do. I observe. And you, my friend, are an impending train wreck."

"I know I compartmentalize, but if I let loose, I'll tear this town apart."

She tilted her head, pursed those lush lips of hers and—no—not going there. Not letting Miss Illinois mess up his thinking. At least not any more than necessary.

"Maybe you *need* to tear this town apart. *Maybe* if you let some of it out, it'll clear your head."

"Ha!" All that festering anger with the lid blown off? He wouldn't know what to do with that hell on earth. She could take her psychological evaluation somewhere else. Finally, the hold music ended and he scooped up the phone, jabbing at the screen and taking it off speaker. "Hello? I need to report a gas leak."

He eyeballed Jenna who eyeballed him right back, then stuck her tongue out at him. Crazy woman. Still, he had to grin. When she returned the smile, he waved her off, but knew he'd have to be careful with her. She had a way of defusing him and he wasn't sure if he was losing his edge or he'd met his match.

After finishing with the operator, Jenna sat two feet in front of him, leaning on her sporty little BMW, her long dark hair pulled over one shoulder, looking like the vixen she was. Time to face facts. He liked her. A lot. And it wasn't just about her looks—although he couldn't complain about them.

He liked the challenge of her. How she questioned every damned thing. Annoying, sure, but fun, too. Call him a masochist.

"They're sending someone out," he said. "Let's head into town and get that ankle x-rayed. By the time we get back, the gas company will be here."

"So that's it? Conversation about your mom is over?"

"Yep." He smacked her on the hip. "Let's get you in the truck."

Ninety minutes and a mild sprain diagnosis later, Brent pulled back into the driveway. A utility truck was parked on the road, but he didn't see any workers. They were here somewhere. "We've got activity."

"All my notes are still in the house. The, uh, photos are on the floor. Just so you know. I didn't get a chance to pick them up. I'll do that now."

He wouldn't object. Having never viewed the photos, he wasn't about to start looking now. "I'll get the crutches for you."

"I don't need them. I can hobble."

"Humor me. Use the crutches for a few days. Your ankle will heal faster."

"Yes, dear," she cracked. "At least I can still drive."

Yeah, like he'd let her drive with a sprained ankle. He'd figure that one out later, but he might be carting her around until that ankle healed enough for her to ditch the crutches. He hopped out of the truck, grabbed the crutches from the backseat and brought them around to her side. Antsy pants already had her door open, ready to go.

He held the crutches up while she slid off the seat, balancing on one foot. "Do you feel comfortable on these?"

"They're fine. If it's clear of gas, I'll be in the house."

"How are you gonna get to the floor?"

She shrugged. "I'll sit on the couch and lean. You worry too much."

"Wha, wha," he said, hanging on to her as she moved across the walkway to the steps. "Hold up. Let me check inside."

The front door was still open—nothing to steal in there but old furniture—and he stuck his head in. No gas that he could detect. He hopped back down the steps. "It's good. Just don't stay in there too long. Get your stuff and get out."

He made sure she got inside then walked around the side of the house where he found a middle-aged guy wearing a neon orange vest with the gas company logo on the back.

"I'm Brent Thompson."

The guy checked a work order that he'd shoved in his back pocket. "You're the owner?"

"Yes."

Technically, his father owned it, but—yeah—not going there.

"I found your problem in the basement." He pointed to the rear of the house where the only entrance to the basement was an exterior door with a broken lock he hadn't gotten around to fixing yet. "It's the furnace. The flexible line leading from the furnace disintegrated. Must be pretty old."

At least twenty-three years. Brent had kept up with basic maintenance on the house, but the furnace? He couldn't remember the last time he'd checked that. Last year maybe, when he'd changed the filter. "Do I need an HVAC repair?"

"Nah. I took care of it. I'm checking a few other things while I'm here, but I think that's the only issue."

That would be welcome news considering his budget couldn't stretch for a repairman. Maintaining two households meant juggling funds. A lot. "Thanks. I'll be inside. Let me know if you need anything."

Inside, he found Jenna on the living room floor studying photos stacked on her lap. If he hadn't shown up earlier than expected, she could be dead right now. Or at least hospitalized.

And he'd have found her. In almost the exact spot where his mother's body had been.

His chest hitched and he rubbed it, digging his fingers in as he pictured shoving that ache down. Down, down, down.

Jenna covered the photos with another file and glanced up. "I'm fine. I couldn't bend with the crutches so I slid down the arm of the couch. It wasn't pretty, but I managed."

"I would have helped you."

"You were busy."

He smiled and then pointed to her lap, letting her know he knew she'd hidden the photos from him. "Thank you."

"You're welcome. How's everything with the gas company?"

He glanced around the room, imagined walking in here and finding yet another woman he cared about on the floor, and that damned hitch in his chest happened again. "How long were you in here before I arrived?"

"Forty-five minutes. Why?"

"Did you see anyone outside?"

"No. But the drapes were closed and I locked the front door. Safety first, you know."

Something wasn't right. He hires an investigator to help him and suddenly, with the investigator in the house, there's a gas leak. Didn't strike him as a coincidence.

"Brent?"

"From now on, I don't want you coming here alone."

She drew her eyebrows together. "Why?"

"Because you were out here alone and there was a gas leak."

"And?"

Miss Illinois was not this dense. Not by a long shot. "It doesn't seem off to you? Like someone doesn't want you in this house."

"Oh, come on. This was a freak thing."

"A freak thing that happened when you were here alone

trying to find a murderer. What are the chances of that? I'd say not good. I'm done talking about it."

She sat on the floor staring up at him, her jean clad legs flat in front of her. "First of all, can you squat down before I get whiplash? Either that or hand me those crutches so I can get up."

He squatted. "There's no discussion. You're not coming here alone."

She shook her head and gave him the you-foolish-boy look. "That'll slow things down, don't you think?"

"Call it collateral damage. I'll live with it."

She scooped up the items on her lap and smacked them against her leg. "I'll pay more attention next time. Even if someone cut that gas line—which I doubt— if I'd opened the drapes, I'd have seen someone outside and could have called for help. I was careless. That's all. Next time I'll open the drapes."

"I don't care."

"Brent! I have a job to do and not being allowed in here will impede that."

Now I'm done squatting. He stood, purposely looming over her because—yeah—he was about to lose this battle and any position of power would do right now. For added effect, he crossed his arms.

"If I showed up later, this could have ended differently."

Now they were getting to the nasty core and his throat burned clear down to his stomach. Dammit. He scratched his head with both hands, really digging in and feeling the pressure. Sexy Jenna Hayward had managed to crack open that long-locked door. He paced the floor, threw open the drapes and stared out. If she pursued this, he was toast. *Let it go.*

"Forget it," he said.

Please. Forget it.

"So, that's what this is about?"

"You're not coming here alone. End of it."

She smacked the photos on the floor. "This may shock you, but that doesn't work for me. You don't get to order me around and expect me to fall in line."

Forget letting it go. The woman never gave up. He spun back to her, jabbed his finger at her. "I don't care what works for you. You're not coming here by yourself."

"Well, *that'll* allow me to get a lot done on your case. Bravo!"

Most annoying woman ever.

As Brent contemplated the many ways he could lose his mind, she picked up one of the crutches and tried to lever off the floor. He took two steps before she banged the crutch against the scarred wood, the sound echoing and bouncing off the walls. "Don't help me. I'm mad at you. You're being pig-headed, and I hate that."

Pig-headed? He'd give her pig-headed. "I'll stand here and watch, then."

Hell, he'd even hum while she struggled to get up. Then, when she finally asked for his help, he'd prove to her she should listen.

He watched as she rolled to her knees, crawled to the couch and dragged the crutches upright. Damned stubborn woman. That acid in his stomach continued frying him. Eventually, using the couch for leverage, she got to her feet and rested on the crutches, staring at him with those unrelenting eyes. She wanted answers. Probably deserved them. But he wasn't going there. Not with her.

Finally, she shook her head. "Are you going to tell me what this is really about?"

Stubborn woman. "No."

"So when my boss asks me how it's going, I'll just tell her that you refuse to let me do my job. That'll go over well considering my firm is doing this pro bono. Nothing like wasting the resources of Chicago's top law firm."

That cracked it. More than cracked it. An explosion of energy shot from his feet straight to his brain. He bent at the waist, breathed in and his eyes throbbed. *Boom, boom, boom.* The pressure might blow his skull apart and he knew it, knew it would be this way. He'd spent his life avoiding this nonsense, avoiding unleashing a storm that would rip this blasted house apart. Well, hell, maybe he needed to unleash it. Why not? She wanted him to talk, he'd talk. He'd do more than that, he'd let her know exactly how he felt. He stepped closer, dipped his head and made direct eye contact.

Keeping his voice low and controlled, hoping she'd finally get the damned point, he said, "I think someone cut that gas line hoping you'd die."

Chapter Five

Jenna opened her mouth, then stopped. As much as she wanted to rail on him, the smarter, wiser Jenna took hold. This man had spent most of his life coping with trauma he'd been unable to find relief from. Now he stood in front of her as if he'd like her to vaporize. Just be gone. Everything about him—the stiff posture, the locked jaw and heavy breathing—all of it screamed anger and hurt and confusion.

"What?" he said, his tone dripping sarcasm. "No snappy comeback?"

She gripped the crutches tighter, willing herself not to take the bait. That's what he wanted. To redirect this conversation. Make it about her and not him and the emotional disaster living inside him. "No, Brent. No snappy comeback." He watched her for a second. *Yeah, big boy, I'm not giving you what you want.* "This isn't my fault. I didn't think about you walking in here and finding me..." She circled the crutch on the floor, but couldn't say it. "I'm sorry for that. But don't bait me into a fight because you're redirecting your anger."

"More psychobabble?"

Oh, he was pushing it. "I don't think someone cut that gas line. It was an accident."

"Ever consider someone might be following you?"

"No. I'm an investigator and these roads are quiet. You don't think I'd have noticed someone following me?"

Brent shook his head. "I'm not arguing with you about this. It's done."

"If you don't want me alone, fine, but with your schedule, you won't be able to pick up and go when I need to. We need a compromise."

Yes. That was it. Bring it back to the case and solving it. From his spot, he eyed her. "What do you propose?"

"I either bring someone with me or have a member of your family here. I can call ahead and make sure they're home, and they can come over with me. That way, I won't be alone and I can still get something done. In fact, Jamie gave me her cell number today. I'm sure she won't mind."

He turned back to the window and shoved the drapes aside. Dust particles flew, but he ignored them and rested one arm along the edge of the frame to stare out. Obviously, he didn't like her compromise but at least he wasn't yelling anymore.

Maneuvering the crutches, she hopped over to him and settled against the wall. "Just think about it. Please."

He rested the side of his face against his arm and dropped into a long, fitful silence. She didn't know what to do. Offer comfort? Stay quiet? Touch him? Don't touch him? What? After a minute that should have been an hour, he lifted his head and focused on her face. His gaze locked with hers and there it was, that heat, that enormous energy that made her think about all the ways she'd like Brent Thompson to be in her life. Maybe he worried too much, but when he went into protection mode, she couldn't help admire him.

"I am thinking about it," he said. "I'd have to talk to my family. I'm not sure how involved they want to be. This is my obsession. Not theirs."

She hooked her hand around his thick biceps, flexed her fingers and shifted closer. *No.* Getting too close wouldn't do either of them any good. She let go of him and instantly mourned the loss. "We can always ask the sheriff."

He shrugged and stared back out the window. "That'd work, I guess. We'd both get what we need."

Had he ever had a day when he'd completely gotten what he needed? Somehow Jenna didn't think so. Not as long as his mother's killer was free.

Boosting off the wall, he faced her, gesturing to the photos and the file she'd left on the floor. "Anything jump out at you?"

For now, she'd let him drop the subject. Emotionally, she was strung out. His exhaustion would be triple hers. So she'd give him what he wanted and return to the puzzle that was his mother's death. As twisted as it seemed, that was apparently Brent's comfort zone.

"I still need to run through all the timelines and talk to that druggie guy you said lived across town. So far, everything your family has told me is consistent with what you've said. And the reports. The druggie is the only one I can't verify a timeline on. Well, and your dad, but Jamie said she saw when your dad pulled in that night and he went crazy. I don't know why I feel this, but I don't think he did it. Can't rule him out, though. I'll need to talk to him."

Brent let out a long breath. "I know. I can give you the last number I had for him, but it's been years. He could be in the wind again."

"I'll find him. For now, let's find this druggie. We'll ask the sheriff to pull any reports of home-invasion incidents from that time. Particularly in surrounding areas. You never know. Something could be related."

"I did that."

"And?"

"Dead end. But I have copies of all the reports at my place. I can give them to you. Fresh eyes, remember?"

She smiled. "I remember. Never hurts to look. I'd also

like to meet with some crime-scene people I know and show them the photos. We need to identify the murder weapon. Or at least get an idea of what it could have been. It might lead us somewhere."

Jenna had helped on a case the prior year where their defendant was accused of killing his brother. He denied it, but their defendant was an avid bowler with plenty of tournament wins. Unfortunately for Penny, that victory wound up going to the prosecution when they found DNA on the base of one of the defendant's trophies—the murder weapon.

Heels clomped against the porch boards and Jenna angled back to find Brent's aunt in the doorway. Sylvie's mouth dropped open. "What on earth is she doing on crutches?"

"She sprained her ankle," Brent said.

"The crutches are a precaution. Your nephew is quite stubborn when he wants to be."

"Oh, honey," Sylvie said, "I could have told you that."

"Aunt Sylvie, don't start. The crutches are a good idea."

Jenna grinned up at him. He simply refused to back down. This was probably the thing that had kept him going on his mother's case all these years.

He tweaked her nose. A nice thing after the blowup they'd just had. At least he didn't hold on to arguments.

"Stop looking at me like that." He smiled down at her. "You all set here? I can run you home in your car and get a lift back with Camille and her husband when they drive out for dinner tonight. I'll drive my car home later."

Right. The family dinner his aunt had guilted him into. But she was not going to have him spending half his day running back and forth.

"That's crazy. My driving foot is fine."

"I know, but it's a long drive. I'd rather take you."

Again they were going to fight? Jenna closed her eyes. A nap would do her some good. "No."

"Yes."

"Or," his aunt said, "the two of you could stop this nonsense and Jenna will stay for dinner. Then you drive her car home, Camille drives yours and Doug drives theirs. Problem solved. We're done here."

This bossy thing must be a family trait. "I don't want to intrude."

"You're not intruding," Brent and his aunt both said. He looked at Sylvie and laughed. "Good one."

"Besides," his aunt said, "it's almost three o'clock. By the time he drives you home and they get back here—because, let's face it, Camille has never been on time a day in her life—my dinner will be ruined. If you stay, I'll get extra time with Brent. I love that idea." Not giving Jenna an inch to argue, the older woman spun to the door. "It's all settled. I'll go to church in the morning, so just pop over to the house when you're done here."

After his aunt left, Jenna flopped out her bottom lip. "Wow."

"Welcome to my life, babe."

"She's downright scary."

He laughed. "Sometimes. But here we are and we've got time to kill. Let's run through your timelines."

JENNA WAS GONE.

The dinner dishes had been cleared and the aroma of his aunt's high-octane coffee drifted into the nook of a dining room where Brent sat with Camille and Jamie discussing everyone's plans for the holidays. Camille and Doug would be gone for Thanksgiving but home for Christmas. Brent, as usual, would either be working—he liked to give the married guys the holidays off—or at his aunt's. No big mystery. Jamie would spend Thanksgiving with her husband's family downstate. Her kids didn't get to see the other set of grandparents often, so they spent the long weekend with them. They'd be back for Christmas, though.

Nope, the only mystery right now was where Jenna had disappeared to. Brent stood and tapped the table. "Be right back."

Camille glanced up, her blue eyes so big and round that it instantly brought him back to childhood and, worse, the teenage years when he'd spent too much time scaring off horny boys. With his father checked out, all of it had fallen on Brent. Someone had to protect Camille, and Brent had never minded watching out for his little sister. Still didn't.

As his sister matured, her looks had changed. Her cheekbones had sharpened and she'd cut her normally long light brown hair to chin length. When she'd done that, her resemblance to their mother had knocked Brent sideways. He couldn't tell Camille, but every time he looked at her, he thought of their mother.

"Where are *you* going?" Camille asked.

"Kitchen. Our guest has gone AWOL."

"You're trying to steal cookies."

He cracked a smile. "Since I'm in the kitchen…"

"Check the cabinet," Jamie said. "I dropped off the pies and a batch of your favorites this morning."

"The chocolate chip? With the macadamias?"

"Yep."

"I love you."

"I know you do, cuz."

He snapped his fingers and spun back in Jamie's direction. "Hey, when you left this morning, did you see anyone?"

"Where?"

"By the house."

She drew in her eyebrows. "Well, there were a few cars on the road, but it's Saturday. People were heading into town. Why?"

"Just curious."

But from the looks of Jamie's hard stare, she wasn't buying it. "Brent, what are you up to?"

Time to bolt. "Nothing. I was curious."

Making his getaway, he strode into the size-impaired kitchen and squeezed between the table and cabinets where his aunt unwrapped two pies.

Brent went straight for the cookie cabinet.

"They're on the table." Aunt Sylvie pointed over her shoulder. "I took them out for you."

There they sat, a good two dozen of his favorite cookies that Aunt Sylvie had taught Jamie how to make. He bent low, kissed his aunt's cheek. "You two are the best."

One thing about his cousin and his aunt, when he was around, they made his favorite foods. How he'd have gotten through his adolescence without their female nurturing and guidance, he'd thankfully never have to know.

"Did you see Jenna?"

"Your uncle said something about a fire. Check out back."

Again with the fire pit? "He's obsessed with that thing."

She sighed. "Don't I know it? He's been this way for years. Did you see he rebuilt it?"

This would be no less than the third time. "Get out."

"He changed out the bricks. Got some fancy ones he picked up in Kentucky."

His uncle was a long-haul trucker who picked up all sorts of junk while on the road. One year he'd come home with enough fireworks to last three years. Another time it had been folding chairs that he'd bought at wholesale prices and resold to townspeople, making a nice profit along the way. When it came to his family, his uncle always made ends meet. No matter what, his family came first.

Brent grabbed three cookies off the plate. "I'm checking out the fire pit."

"Two cookies, Brent. Save room for pie."

"Whoops. Already touched the third one. Have to take it now." Knowing her kill zone, he grinned. "Isn't that what you always told me?"

"Don't sass me." She shooed him from the cookies. "Go."

He gave her a backward wave, pushed open the storm door and found his uncle sitting across from a blanket-wrapped Jenna in front of a roaring fire. A cool wind blew the smell of burning timber toward him and he breathed in. Nice. In the two hours he'd been inside, the temperature had dropped a good ten degrees. The cooler air smacked at his cheeks. He'd left his jacket inside so his long-sleeved T-shirt would have to do. "Hey, nice fire pit."

"Picked up the bricks a couple of weeks ago. Home improvement store going out of business. Helluva deal."

To Brent, they just looked like bricks. He grabbed one of the aluminum patio chairs and, hoping to hell the thing would hold him, set it next to Jenna's. She'd propped her foot up on a cinder block that had been sitting in the yard for ten years.

"How's the ankle?"

"It's okay. Better now that it's propped up."

"That cinder block is good for something at least."

"Don't make fun of my cinder block," Uncle Herb shot back. "She's got her foot up on it, doesn't she?"

Jenna made a hissing sound. "Got you there, big boy."

At that, Brent made the mistake of looking at her and—*pow*—there it was again, that crazy feeling he got in his chest every time she came within five feet of him. And with the heat from the fire, the flames lighting up her face and shining off her long dark hair, she was nothing short of movie-star stunning. Their gazes held and, well, truth of it was, they stunk at this no-flirting thing. He knew it, his erection knew it and apparently his uncle also knew it, because Herb cleared his throat and made some lame excuse to go inside.

Brent watched him go, suddenly not sad to be alone with Jenna in front of a fire. "Coffee is almost ready. Then we'll head out."

"No rush."

"Camille likes to get out fast." He broke the amazing eye contact and studied the conjoined yards where all the open space had provided plenty of running room when he was a kid. "She's never said it, but being here throws her."

"It's understandable. I'm not family and knowing what happened next door throws *me*."

A hunk of wood in the fire snapped and they sat in silence while it crackled and broke apart. Jenna set her foot on the ground and shifted to him. "Can you get me the contact information for that other suspect? I'd like to check him out tomorrow."

"I have it at home. If you can wait until afternoon, I'll drive you. He lives about an hour from here."

"Do you have time for that?"

"Yeah. It's Sunday. Unless something comes up, I'm off. I've got a game with a bunch of guys in the morning, but we're usually done by eleven."

"That sounds fun."

"It is fun. I miss football."

"Maybe I'll come watch. Then we can go right from there. Unless it's a guy thing."

"Not at all. Some of the guys bring their kids. You can be my plus one."

Jenna sighed. "I hate that plus-one thing. And right now it feels like everyone is getting married or having some kind of function, and I keep getting these invitations with Jenna Hayward and guest."

He knew that feeling. "Annoying, isn't it?"

"Thank you! I know people are being nice, in case

there's someone I want to bring, but it's like a pressure thing. I know I'm crazy, but that's how it feels."

"It's not crazy." He jerked his thumb at the door. "I get it all the time from the crew inside. *When are you getting married? Who are you dating? I met a nice girl at the market.* It never ends."

Between his hours on the job and his mom's case, he didn't have time to date. All he had were two hours on Sunday when he played football to work off the damned stress of his life. He considered that a mental-health necessity. Football was the release valve. Well, sex too, but since he wasn't getting too much of that lately, football would have to do.

"I never get that from my family. I have four brothers, though, and a father who cleans his gun when I bring dates around."

Brent laughed. "That'll be me one day."

"I think my father and brothers would be happy if I joined a convent. They've hated all my boyfriends."

"They hate them because they love you. I hated Doug, too. And he's the nicest guy I know. I just didn't want him having sex with my sister. Hell, they're married and I still don't want him having sex with her. Ew."

Jenna reached over and poked him, her long nail digging into his arm before she backed away again. "See, I love that about *you*, but I hate it about my family."

"It's what brothers do. I've always taken care of Camille. She lost her mom."

"So did you."

"Yeah, but she's a girl and girls need a mom."

"So do boys."

He waggled his hand at her. Enough said on that front. "Tomorrow, I'll pick you up about 8:30 a.m. We'll go to my game and then head out to see one Terrence Jeffries. I'll need a shower before, but I'll buy you lunch while you wait."

"It'll give me time to study your notes. Do you think there's anything there?"

If there was, he couldn't find it. "Jeffries says he was home alone that night."

"What's your gut saying?"

"My gut says it's not him. I can't go by that, though. This is my mother. I second-guess everything."

"You're too close to it."

"That's why I have you."

Again, she leaned over, but this time touched his knee. "I'll do whatever I have to. I wanted this before, but after spending time with you and your family, my reasons are different. You all need closure. I want to help you get it."

He stared down at her hand on his knee and his pulse went ballistic. Off-the-charts ballistic. Not to mention the erection he was sporting. Female friends casually touched him all the time. This, right here, the way his body responded? It had been months since he'd felt that. Damn, he needed sex. And suddenly, his typical one-nighters that got the job done—the means to an end—wouldn't do.

He'd been thinking about Jenna Hayward in a less than gentlemanly way since the day he'd met her. And something told him if he pursued it, they'd both be willing participants.

But they'd agreed no funny stuff.

At least until her work on his mother's case was over.

Have to wait. For now. He grabbed her hand, gave it a gentle squeeze, then stood. "We should head inside."

Scooping her crutches off the ground, he held them with one hand and extended his other to help her up.

"Thank you."

He set the crutches in front of her. "You good here?"

"Yep."

He waved her ahead of him, but she stopped. "What?"

"You're always taking care of people. Makes me wonder who takes care of you."

Once again. *Pow.* Right in the chest. She hobbled to the door and waited for him to open it while he tried to string together a sentence. He got there, set his hand on the knob, but didn't open it. "I don't think about it."

"I know. Maybe, when this is over, we can change that."

Chapter Six

The next morning, after watching Brent and his over-amped friends nearly kill each other on a football field, Jenna rode shotgun to pay a surprise visit to Terrence Jeffries. Who knew if he'd be home, but she couldn't worry about that. One thing she didn't want was to alert him that they were coming so he could take off. If he wound up not being home, they'd wait. And wait a little more until he arrived.

Brent merged his SUV onto the tollway and hit the gas. Traffic was light and apparently that worked for Brent because he set the cruise control and let his fingers do the driving.

Jenna turned sideways to face him. "So, you maniacs play that hard every Sunday and no one winds up in a hospital?"

"Sometimes. But that's football."

"I mean, when you said football, I was thinking flag or touch. You boys were in full pads."

"Yeah. We're all ex college or high-school players who miss the adrenaline rush."

"That's insanity."

He made a *pffting* sound. "That's stress relief."

Oh, brilliant. "Of course. You look at the guy across from you and then slam him to the ground. And then, for kicks, he does it back."

He glanced at her and grinned. "What's your point?"

"I guess I don't have one."

Except, as much as the roughness made her wince, there was something rather delicious about seeing Brent Thompson in his tight football pants, tearing his way through a defensive line to their quarterback. Simple fact: this man possessed an uncontainable hotness. The scarf around her neck—a pretty yellow one her mom had given her— became too much and she tugged on it, letting air hit her neck. Brent shifted his grip on the steering wheel and she studied his long fingers. Talented fingers. Probably in more ways than one.

Oh, boy. She loosened the scarf a little more. This line of thinking wouldn't serve either one of them. Not after that moment by the fire pit last night when she seriously wanted to jump him. She faced front again and dug in her briefcase for a file.

"Terrence Jeffries. Have you ever questioned him?"

"Me personally? No. I've given the sheriff questions, though, and he's spoken to him many times. He's good at talking his way around an interview, which is amazing considering he's been stoned for thirty years."

"Still, huh?"

Brent shrugged. "As far as I know."

"Okay. I'm going in there playing the new-girl card. I'll tell him I'm new on the case and just wanted to hear from him where he was that night. Maybe he'll slip up."

"I'll wait outside. My presence won't help you."

"He doesn't like you?"

"He knows he's a suspect in my mother's murder. That alone makes him not like me."

She held up the file and flicked it. "Good point."

"I'll be outside if you need me."

"I know you will."

Seventy-five long miles later, Brent parked in front of

a faded white, broken-down cottage. A Jeep with rusted wheels sat in the tiny driveway. Jenna took that as a good sign.

"Nice place."

"He invests his money in drugs."

Leaving the crutches in the car, Jenna limped to the front door with Brent on her heels. He stopped at the bottom of the steps leading to the stone porch. "I don't understand why you won't use crutches."

"I am using them. Just not right now."

He shook his head. "Whatever. I'll be right here."

"I'll holler if I need you."

"Last time I saw this guy he weighed about ninety pounds. Even with a bum ankle, you could take him."

She knocked on the door and faced front so Mr. Jeffries would get a face full of Jenna and not Brent standing at the base of the stairs. She turned back to him. "Maybe you should scoot to the side so he doesn't see you. At least until I get in there."

"Nope. He needs to know you're not alone."

"I'll be fine."

"And I'll be right here."

The front door swung open and a tall, thin man with gray—literally—skin stood there. What was left of his hair stuck up on one side, and a half-smoked cigarette hung from his mouth. The notes in the evidence file said he'd been twenty-two when the murder occurred. Jeffries looked a whole lot older than forty-five, but a life of drugs did that to a body. Tore it down, weakened and aged it.

Time to put the Miss Illinois Runner-Up smile to work. "Hello. I'm Jenna Hayward."

He gave her the standard once-over, checking her out from head to toe. After Brent's comment the other day about not selling herself short with revealing clothing, she'd opted to test his theory and went with jeans, a T-shirt and a blazer. Even so, the look Jeffries gave her spoke volumes about where his mind had gone. Nothing unusual there. At least until he spotted Brent at the base of the stairs.

"Oh, come on, man," he said. "I keep telling you I didn't hurt your mother."

Needing to refocus Jeffries, Jenna took two steps sideways and blocked his view of Brent. "I'm an investigator helping out with the investigation into Mrs. Thompson's death. Your name is in the file."

"Yeah, because they think I did it. And I keep saying I didn't."

"Which is why I'd like to ask you a few questions. To see if we can rule you out."

He craned his neck to see Brent.

"He'll wait right there," Jenna said. "I'm the only one talking to you."

"Are you a cop? My lawyer says I shouldn't talk to cops without him."

A smart man, your lawyer. "I'm not a cop. As I said, I'm a private investigator. I work for a law firm, and we're helping with the investigation." That's all she'd give him. If he chose to talk to her and she discovered something to turn over to police, it was still his choice to speak with her. Even if it was hearsay, information communicated by someone else and not verifiable, a smart prosecutor could find a way to make it admissible. Jenna waited while Jeffries glanced at Brent and then back to her.

"I need to call my lawyer." He stepped back. "You can come in if you want. Or stand there. I don't care."

He spun away from her, leaving the front door open. Oh, she was going in. If nothing else, simply to eavesdrop on the conversation with his lawyer. "If you don't mind, I'll step in. It's rather windy out here."

"Leave the door open," Brent said from the bottom of the steps.

She glanced back at him, gave him a discreet thumbs-up, but he climbed the two steps and leaned against the porch pole, keeping her in sight.

Inside, the living room was a small, perfectly square room with a twenty-inch television sitting on a wooden folding tray. Across from it were a patched plaid sofa that had to be someone's great-grandma's and an end table with a cheap ceramic lamp. Above the sofa two shelves held what looked like sports memorabilia. Interesting. Jenna peeked down the hall where Jeffries's voice drifted from another room. Bedroom maybe.

Knowing Brent watched, she jerked her head toward the wall and then wandered to where the collection of sports items—broken bats, a deflated football, a yellow flag, a signed ball—gathered dust. Next to the broken bat was a hunk of cement. She snapped photos of the items. Once she was through, she glanced down the hall. No sign of Jeffries. Good, because she wanted a closer look at the cement. Using her scarf as a glove, she pulled it down and studied it for signs of dried blood. Twenty-three years later, who knew if it might still be possible, but she'd learned to note everything. She set it on the floor and took pictures from different angles. Couldn't hurt to compare the shape to the crime scene photos of the wounds on Brent's mother.

A long shot at best. This would be one dumb killer to leave a murder weapon out in the open. She placed the items back in their original positions on the shelf. The dust was disturbed, but hopefully she'd be gone by the time he noticed. If not, she'd talk her way out of it. A little eye-batting and smiling could take a girl anywhere.

Jeffries shuffled back to her, his head down. "My lawyer's service can't find him. They found his partner, and he said I shouldn't talk to anyone without a lawyer. We should set up an appointment."

Of course they should. Jenna dug into her purse. "That

would be fine. As I said, I'm just verifying a few things. Here's my card. Have your lawyer contact me."

He took the card. "We'll call you."

Liar. But if they didn't, she'd come back. And she'd keep coming back—and calling—until he agreed to talk to her. "Great."

She held her hand out and he shook it. "She was a nice lady. I didn't do it."

"Then you won't mind answering my questions. With your lawyer."

STANDING OUTSIDE TERRENCE JEFFRIES'S house was not on Brent's list of favorite things to do. Ideally, assuming the guy was the murderer who'd ripped Brent's life away, Brent wanted to crush his skull. Make the guy feel what Brent's mother had while blood had poured out of her. When she'd known her children would find her body.

But if the man was innocent, that skull bashing would be a problem. Thus, he stayed away from Terrence Jeffries. Too many conflicting emotions. Too much anger.

Too much pain.

Hearing Jenna say goodbye to Jeffries, Brent boosted off the porch pole and walked down the steps to wait for her.

She exited the house, pulled the door closed and hobbled toward him, her lush body moving as fast as her bum ankle would let her.

"Let's go. I've got photos to print and compare to the crime-scene ones."

Years of dead ends had taught him to keep his hopes in check, but the excitement in her eyes, the energy coming off her, she had something. "What photos? You found something?"

She grabbed his forearm and dragged him to the car. "I'll show you in the car. He's got all sorts of sports memorabilia. Bats, balls, that kind of stuff. But he also has a hunk of cement. I don't know what it is, but I snapped pictures."

Ah, damn. Here she was all pumped about her discovery and he'd have to wreck it. They reached his SUV and Brent opened the door, letting her slide in before propping his arm on the door frame.

"What?" Jenna said.

"The cement. It's a piece of an old baseball stadium that was torn down. In 2008."

Jenna's body deflated. *Boom.* That fast, her excitement faded. He knew the feeling.

She smacked her palms against her thighs. "Well, shoot."

"It came up when the sheriff questioned him a few years ago. There's nothing there."

Jenna grasped the front of his shirt and gently tugged. "I'm so sorry."

"For what?"

"I thought I had something. Now I've dragged you all the way out here to tell you what you already knew."

He leaned in closer and got to eye level with her. "Hey, you're doing exactly what I need you to. Fresh eyes, Jenna. I don't care if we go through every piece of evidence again. You might see something differently, and that's what we need. Don't get down on yourself. We knew going in this wouldn't be easy and you've just started. So lighten up." He grinned. "Don't be a baby."

"Hey!" She twisted his shirt in her fist and he set his hand over hers.

"I was teasing."

Untangling their hands, she played with his fingers, gently stroking each one—*hello, erection*—until she got to his pinky. What the hell had he been thinking putting his hands on her? Huge mistake. Sex-starved as his body was, he should have known better than to reach into that cookie jar. Considering he was a man who liked cookies.

He backed away, straightened up. "This is killing me. We should go."

"Brent…" she began, her voice low and husky.

He'd bet she sounded that way in the morning, when she woke up from a long night in the sack. Immediately, his mind drifted to Jenna—naked—in a bed, legs tangled in sheets. Dammit. Even her voice made him crazy. That may have been his desperate body talking, though.

"No, Jenna. We…we need to go. Before I do something stupid. Something we both agreed wouldn't happen. Let's just…" *Find a room.* "…go. We *need* to go."

Not bothering to look back at Jeffries's house, because, yeah, that would only aggravate him more, Brent made his way around the front of the SUV.

His bum luck that his surefire release of aggravation was sex. Lots of it. And right now, on his day off when he had plenty of time for that particular endeavor, his boiling attraction to Jenna, combined with not being able to crush Terrence Jeffries's skull, might turn him into a maniac.

He hopped into the driver's side and kept his eyes straight ahead. *Don't look at the hot brunette.* Three blocks later, they still sat in silence, but he was in no rush for conversation. Speaking to her, like touching her, would be trouble.

"Are you mad?" she asked.

And didn't that blow the whole not-speaking-to-her plan? "No. I'm…" He slapped his hand over his mouth and dragged it down.

Driving right now would be a mistake. He parked in front of a clump of trees, sat back and organized his thoughts. All the thinking about not having sex only made him want to have sex. Time to have this conversation. But then he'd have to look at her. Always trouble. *Suck it up.*

He released the seat belt, shifted sideways and, yep, that thumping in his chest started right up. "I don't know what

I am. I want things. None of which I can have right now and it's…frustrating."

"I know, but we'll get there."

What? Did she have any idea he was talking about them spending excessive time in a bed? If so, she was pretty damned open about it.

No.

She had to be talking about the case. The no-flirting rule was her brilliant idea and she'd better not be taunting him with the idea they'd eventually get busy. "Uh, I think we're talking about different things."

"No, it'll be fine." She tapped her phone. "Even if these photos aren't of the murder weapons, I can compare them to the pictures of your…the pictures from that night. I'll see if there are any similarities. So this trip wasn't a waste. Don't be frustrated."

Ha. Kicker, that. She thought he was frustrated about the memorabilia. *That* came and went four years ago when the issue first came up.

Unable to resist, he ran his index finger along her cheek. "Honey, I'm not talking about the pictures."

Brent waited for his meaning to penetrate. *One, two…*

"Ooohhh," she said.

And, God, her lips were perfect. Just puffy enough that he'd like to stroke his thumb across the bottom one and feel all that softness. Kissable lips. Exceptionally kissable lips.

And it hurt.

Looking at her had become an exercise in torture. He wanted her. Plain and simple. Whether that want would go away after a few hours of fun—as usually happened—he couldn't be sure. *This* wanting, the one keeping him up at night, felt different. Rooted. Like it wouldn't die with fast, primal sex.

What he didn't need was a woman getting inside his head and staying there. His adult existence had consisted of finding his mother's killer. It was, in fact, all he knew—emotionally speaking. He had no room for anything else. No room. Zero.

When he found the killer, maybe then. Now? No way. He'd blow off his own head trying to juggle a relationship with his mom's case.

But Jenna was looking at him with those amazing blue eyes and that punch to the chest ripped his air away. *Hell with it.*

He kissed her.

Not gently, either. When his lips hit hers, months of need broke loose. She didn't protest. Unless her tongue in his mouth was meant to be a protest. He didn't think so. He leaned in, nipped at the bottom lip he'd just fantasized about and she made a sound, a half groan, half moan low in her throat that set every nerve in his body blazing.

She clamped her hand around the back of his neck and held him there, angled her body closer and—uh—he didn't know what to do with his hands. He knew what he wanted to do, but his brain had stalled. Overload.

So he backed up. *Seriously?*

"Hang on," he said.

But she was focused on his lips and inched closer, moving in for round two. Had she heard him?

"Hey!" he hollered. "Unless you want me to find the nearest hotel, we've got to stop. I can't take it. I'm trying to do the right thing here. The *thing* you said you wanted. Or, in this case, didn't want, but I'm still a *guy* who *likes* sex. A lot. So I'm not sticking with this doing-the-right-thing long. Decide what you want, Jenna, and I'll give it to you."

Finally, her gaze drifted from his lips, up to his eyes. She blinked. Three times.

"I want us to be clear on what we're doing," he continued. "Are we clear?"

With the heat incinerating the car, it took her a second, but she nodded. "We shouldn't tempt ourselves, right?"

"If that's what you want, yes."

"I want both. That's the problem. I want everything."

Ha. Didn't everyone. "Yeah, well, sometimes life sucks."

"That it does." She rested her head back against the seat and stared out the windshield. "I guess we should head home, then."

"I guess we should."

"Brent?"

"What?"

"I think I'm crazy about you."

He jammed the stupid seat belt into the buckle and looked over at her. This was a message he needed to deliver while staring her right in the face. No avoidance.

"That's good, because I think I'm crazy about you, too. But I don't have room for a relationship. I don't want to hurt you. You have to know that. Every relationship I've had has ended badly. I'm too wrapped up in finding my mother's killer. Women always start out admiring that, but when I break dates or bail on functions to chase a lead, they get pissed. I don't blame them, but there's nothing I can do about it. I owe my mother this. I owe my family this. It comes first, always."

"And I'm high-maintenance."

"I didn't say that."

"I know I need a lot of stroking—it's part of me—and you don't have time for stroking."

"I did *not* say that."

And here we go. They weren't even *in* a relationship and they were arguing about the very thing he wanted to avoid.

Jenna held up her hands. "I'm stating the obvious. We don't have to debate it." She reached over and squeezed his arm. "Please. I'm not mad. Honesty shouldn't be a bad thing. The truth we can work with."

Extraordinary woman. He sat back in his seat, blew out a breath. She'd given him the out. Let him off the hook. So why didn't it feel good? The sense of relief he should feel didn't materialize. All he felt was bottled up. Like a pop needing to explode.

"I care about you," he said. "And whatever this is going on with us, I like it. It drives me insane, but I like it. We should wait until you're off my mom's case, though. Not complicate things."

"Of course. By then we'll probably be sick of each other."

Doubtful. Another thing that scared the hell out of him.

Chapter Seven

Jenna pushed through her apartment door and headed straight for her computer. Behind her, Brent trailed along so she waved him to a chair—any chair—while she downloaded the photos.

"Have a seat. If you want something from the kitchen, help yourself."

Because I'm in work mode and not playing hostess.

Despite the cement being ruled out as a murder weapon, there was something tugging at her. She needed to study the photos, compare them to the crime-scene pics and let her brain absorb it all. Sometimes, sitting in the quiet, just *being*, brought everything into sharper focus.

What she was focusing on, she wasn't certain, but it was in there somewhere. And she'd find it. For Brent, for his mom and family, for her career, she'd find it.

She plugged her phone into the laptop, booted up and waited.

From the corner of her eye, she saw Brent drop onto her sofa. He'd avoided the side chair that, when it came to his giant frame, looked like a baby seat.

"What's your plan?" he asked.

"I'm printing the photos to study them." Laptop still cooking, she swiveled her chair toward him. The man was simply huge and with all that hugeness came a sense of…

what? Not comfort because this was her space, her sanctuary that she'd decorated to the tiniest detail. Every muted color, every rich fabric, every quirky photo was her doing. Even the finish on the hardwood was chosen by her. All of it imperfectly coordinated to create a home that from the second she walked into it made her feel warmth and satisfaction and happiness. Her space.

That now had a very large man in it. A very large man she could see in it for a long time to come.

If she let herself.

Brent Thompson was a war zone. That or he was a coward, which she didn't believe. This was the guy so emotionally damaged that he closed in on himself and refused to let anyone new in.

And she wanted him. The guy she couldn't have.

Obviously, that unbelievable kiss had turned her stupid.

Her laptop dinged and she whipped back to it. Better that than thinking about Brent and her and the relationship she'd like to try.

Behind her, she heard him move, and then he was beside her. The soft, clean scent of soap from his earlier shower reached her, somehow settling her.

This was a destructive path. He'd flat out told her so. What was wrong with her? She was a walking cliché of love-the-man-you-can't-have. Well, too bad.

"I'm sorry, but I like having you around."

She kept her eyes on the laptop because looking up at the giant hunk behind her wouldn't help her current level of stupidity.

"That's a bad thing?" he asked.

"No."

"Then why are you apologizing?"

"Because you don't want me to like it." She clicked on

the series of photos to print. "You want me to push you away."

He sighed. "I never said that."

I'm such a cliché. "Ignore me. We had an agreement and I'm blowing it. I don't want that."

Humming noises came from the printer and she rolled her chair sideways to retrieve the photos. Except he moved with her and squatted beside her, that clean soapy smell right there, in her face, making her want to curl up in him.

"Hey."

Jenna focused on her photos. Underneath all her talk about waiting until the case was over, she knew she was a liar. She enjoyed his company, enjoyed the way he took care of everyone around him, enjoyed that smile he hit her with just before he was about to tease her about something. All of it. She wanted it. Even the damaged parts, because those were the parts—each annoying, heartbreaking component—that made him into *this* man.

"No, Brent."

Slowly, he swiveled her chair to face him, but she kept her gaze down, pretending to study the photos because— darn it—if she looked at him, she'd make a fool of herself.

"We said we'd be honest, right?"

Oh, such a man, throwing her words back at her. Now she *had* to look at him. Or slap him. It was a toss-up as to which would actually happen.

"Yes. I think we're both painfully clear on that. I shouldn't have said anything. It was a statement of fact that has suddenly spun out of my control because—" she threw up her hands "—guess what? I happen to care about you and I don't want to feel like I shouldn't. There. Said it. Now I'm done."

"Whoa! Who's making you feel like you shouldn't?"

"You. Me. Both of us. You don't want a relationship.

That's fine, but it doesn't mean I can't care about you and enjoy your company. If there's one message I've received it is that you *will* walk away. You said it yourself."

Oh, Jenna. So stupid.

He'd told her he'd walk, that he'd leave her, he'd set the stage for his grand exit, yet here she was, wanting what she shouldn't.

"Hang on," he said. "All I asked was if we could wait until you were done working my mother's case. That's all. I need the two areas separate so I don't get distracted and miss something."

"You don't actually believe this garbage you sell yourself, do you?"

He stood, looming over her, and she popped out of her chair, squared off with him even though she barely reached his shoulder.

"What the hell are you talking about?"

"You're so emotionally closed off, you're hollow. Or you like to think you are."

He flinched. Good. At last, an unrehearsed reaction.

"Finally using that psychology degree, huh? Beauty queen turned detective-slash-shrink. Classic, Jenna."

She stepped back, a little stung from the jab. *Wow.* "Now we're getting somewhere."

"Nowhere good. That's for sure."

He grabbed his jacket off the back of the chair and headed for the door. Leaving. Of course. The minute she started dismantling the armor, he wanted to run. Talk about a cliché.

"That's the difference between us," she said. "I see this conversation as an opportunity to talk about the hurt and anger you've bottled up for twenty-three years. You see it as an attack."

He stood in the doorway with his back to her, his jacket

clutched in one hand, his fingers working the fabric. Finally, he glanced back. "What is it you want from me?"

"That's the problem, Brent. I want what you can't give me."

"We talked about this!" he hollered. "You said you were fine with waiting until you were done on this case."

"And I am."

"Then what are we fighting about?"

She folded her arms, checked herself. Focused on not screaming, not falling into the scenario he'd obviously learned to manipulate with other women. Suddenly, she saw it all, could envision him having this argument over and over again, the woman in front of him desperately trying to break through the wall that was Brent. Each time it probably started and ended with the woman asking him to love her and him apologizing. Oh, he was brilliant. As in any football game, he'd figured out the plays that would get him the result he needed.

The one that allowed him to walk away.

Well, she wasn't giving it to him. *Sorry.* "You think this is about me wanting a relationship. It's not."

He gawked. "I'm confused."

"What I want is for you to feel something. Or at least admit you're afraid to."

"Honey," he said, loading her up on the sarcasm as he stepped into the hallway, "you're not getting either."

BRENT HUSTLED DOWN the front steps of the three-flat Jenna lived in on Chicago's west side. A few kids were messing with a soccer ball by one of the huge trees lining the sidewalk. He angled around them as he passed the tightly packed row of houses. He'd parked two blocks down because—yeah—this was Chicago and on-street parking was a challenge.

The walk would do him good. He could stomp his way

down the block to relieve his aggravation. With his luck, he'd blow out a knee. He eased up on the stomping and sucked in a deep breath. Moisture hung in the air and the temperature had dropped into the fifties, but for him, right now, he needed the cool air hitting his lungs. Perfection. He lengthened his stride—ah, to heck with it—he had sneakers on, he'd run the two blocks, get his heart rate up and bust off some anger. Perfect weather for it.

Freaking women. Always hassling him. Every time. If he was honest, it backfired on him. If he wasn't honest, it backfired. Either way, it never worked and the slew of women in his wake could all attest to it.

And now this one. She thought she could get inside his head a different way. Not happening. It all came down to the same thing. They wanted something he couldn't give.

He hit the button on his key ring and hopped into the SUV. Damn, Jenna. He'd thought he would have it made with her. She understood him. At least he thought. Until she hit him with this psyche mumbo jumbo. What the hell was that?

His phone rang. This would be her. Wanting to *talk*. He should just video these episodes and play them for the women who came into his life. He'd call it the warning video.

The phone rang again and he ripped it out of his jacket. "What?"

"Whoa." Male voice. "Your social skills need work."

"Russ?"

Special agent Russ Voight from the FBI's Chicago field office had been the agent on a fraud case involving one of Penny's clients. The same case where Brent had been assigned to provide security for Penny. In a truly bizarre—or maybe not so bizarre—way, Russ and Penny had managed to explore the personal side of their relationship and were currently in talks about an engagement. Well, Penny was talking. Russ was listening. One thing about Russ, he wouldn't be rushed into anything.

At the end of that grueling fraud case, Brent and Russ had found themselves friends. Facing death together had created a bond between them. Not that they talked about it. It just was what it was.

It didn't hurt that they were both rabid fans of any Chicago sports team and occasionally met for beers to take in a game.

"You okay?" Russ asked.

No. "Yeah. I'm good. In the middle of something. What's up?"

"Bears are getting destroyed."

Dammit. Missed the Bears game. Brent fired the engine and flipped to the game on the radio. "That bad?"

"You're not watching? Wise. Save yourself the agony."

"I've been running around with Jenna."

"How's that going?"

"Ha!"

Russ laughed. "Ouch. Bud, that doesn't sound good."

"She's a handful."

"That she is. Usually Jenna being a handful works in Penny's favor. You may have noticed, she never gives up."

Brent noticed. "That's a plus. Most times."

"Dude, what the hell is wrong with you? You sound like a whiny five-year-old."

He *felt* like a whiny five-year-old.

"I don't know." He scrubbed a hand over his face. "Women confuse me. I mean, I'm honest and I get in trouble. If I'm not honest, I get in trouble. I don't understand what the entire female population wants from me."

"You think that makes you special? You're not. None of us know. What happened?"

Brent snorted. Having this conversation with Russ? Please. He'd rather amputate his own toe. "It's stupid."

"Probably."

"Nice. Is this your sensitive side?"

"No. I save that for Penny. I have to keep it in reserve."

At that, Brent laughed. Men were easier to deal with. No hidden messages, no guesswork. If you thought a guy was dumb, you said he was dumb and everyone moved on.

"It shouldn't be this difficult to understand women. I mean, I told her straight away what the deal was."

"Jenna? What *deal*?"

He couldn't tell Russ. Couldn't. Russ would tell Penny, and she'd go ballistic and accuse him, like every other male who looked at a female twice, of being a pig. But he was so mad that if he didn't blow off some of this, he'd explode.

A guy pulled up beside him, pointed at the SUV. *Parking space.* Not happening. Brent knew his temper and driving all churned up like this would not end well. He waved the guy on and cut the engine so it didn't look as if he would be pulling out.

Theoretically, Russ might understand the Jenna situation. He'd gotten involved with Penny during a case and that had to be dicey, considering it was his case and Penny was the defense lawyer.

"Okay. But you need to let me finish. Hear me out and then—"

"You slept with her. You've got to be kidding me."

"No. I just said let me finish."

"When you start like that, where's my mind supposed to go?"

Point there. "I didn't sleep with her, although, that thought hasn't escaped me. I'm not blind. But we've got this..." He waved one hand in the air, searching for the word. "...energy. It's getting in the way."

"I know that energy."

"Exactly. But here I think I'm being a good guy by telling her my personal life doesn't exist until I figure out what happened with my mom, and it blows up on me."

"You said that?"

"In a nice way, yeah."

"Huh," Russ said. "Can't imagine why she's upset."

"Hey, I didn't say it was right, but at least I'm honest. What do these women want from me?"

I want you to feel something. That's what Jenna had said.

"Uh, your time?"

"Which I don't have."

Russ sighed. "Look, don't get agitated, but if this happens a lot—"

"All the time!"

"Then you gotta wonder if it's not you and change your approach."

Brent slammed his hand on the steering wheel. "I'm being honest."

"And I appreciate that. I'm just saying there might be more to this than you want to acknowledge."

Or at least admit you're scared.

Dammit. Every line she'd laid on him was looping in his head. He needed to break that loop. Rip it to pieces. Fast.

"Did I lose you?" Russ asked.

"No. I'm here."

"Jenna's a great girl. Penny loves her. But she needs a certain amount of positive reinforcement. She's at her best when people love her. If you choose to get involved, you'd better be able to give her what she needs. That's how this works. You get what you need. She gets what she needs. With Penny, it's easy. I keep her stocked in white gummy bears and she knows I love her. I just sat through a Bears game sorting gummy bears. If you'd ever asked me if I'd do that, I'd have flattened you. But here I am."

Brent rested his head back and dug his thumb and middle

finger into his eyes. All this talking about not talking wore him out. And he wasn't even close to done with this topic.

"Jenna *is* great. Amazing even. She's the first woman in a long time I think I could actually…" *Love*. No. Not love. Nuh-uh. "I don't know. Something."

"You need to talk to her."

"And say what?"

He knew. Down deep, in those nasty places he didn't dwell on, he knew she terrified him.

"Wha, wha. How the hell should I know? But if you didn't care, you'd have forgotten about it by now. Talk to her."

"Dude!"

"Dude!" Russ hollered back.

Despite his foul mood, Brent smiled. Once again, guys were easy. "I gotta think about how to do this without losing my man card."

Russ laughed. "You do that. I'm coming downtown to meet Penny for dinner. She's running late—shocker, that. Meet me for a beer and we'll talk sports."

That wasn't a bad idea. Sports was a nice, low impact topic that would distract him from all this other emotional nonsense.

Women.

His entire life consisted of either losing them or fighting with them. No wonder he was still single.

Chapter Eight

There had been record-setting trips to Carlisle before, but this one may have been the topper. Forty-three minutes. After his aunt had called him asking why Jenna was in Carlisle without him, Brent decided that was a great question, ditched Russ and the beer he'd been nursing for an hour and headed south. He'd hit the left lane and off he'd gone. He'd love to know what the hell Jenna was doing traipsing through his house with the sheriff. At least she hadn't gone back on her word to not go there alone. That might be the only thing keeping him from blowing his stack.

For a second, he'd considered calling her, but had nixed that. At the time, he wasn't ready for another round of arguing. Still wasn't, but if he concentrated on his mom's case, like he always did, he could keep everything in check.

He swung into the driveway and parked behind the sheriff's cruiser and Jenna's BMW. To his left, Aunt Sylvie had obviously been doing her eagle-eye routine and was now heading toward him. Great. All he wanted was to get inside and see what the hell was going on, and now he had his aunt detaining him.

He met her on the patch of grass between the two houses, and they stood in the dark where the spotlights from both homes didn't quite reach.

"Hi," she said. "You drove too fast."

He kissed her cheek and the scent of cooking meat—dinner—lingered on her, reminding him that he hadn't eaten yet. "Yell at me later. Let me see what's going on inside and I'll update you."

"Do you think they've found something?"

She's worried. Or simply agitated over the sudden activity at her sister's house. He wrapped her in a hug, gave her the good, solid squeeze she loved. "I don't know. Don't get ahead of yourself. Let me see what's what. It could be nothing."

"I'm scared, Brent."

Me, too.

He backed away, held her at arm's length. "I know."

"I don't know if I can take another disappointment."

That, he understood. All too well. "I have a good feeling this time. Maybe we'll get a break and we'll finally let Mom rest." He jerked his head. "Go inside. I'll update you in a few."

Aunt Sylvie glanced up at the house where light seeped through the drapes. A shadow crossed through the slit and Brent's stomach seized.

Combining the activity around the house with the Jenna-torment left his ability to compartmentalize a crumbling mess. He was most definitely coming apart.

Coming apart. Seriously? Was he a crybaby now? All this psychobabble worming around his head might make him crazier than he'd ever be on his own. He tilted up his head, stared at the few twinkling stars and let the quiet night settle his mind.

He closed his eyes and cracked his neck. *Get to work.*

On the porch, he hesitated. Go in? Knock first? His damned house and he was knocking? Not. At the same time, Jenna hadn't told him she'd be coming out. Whether that was because of their argument or because she didn't want him to see what they were doing, he didn't know.

And he didn't like not knowing.

Having her rifle through his life and rip it open was his idea. He'd practically demanded that she be bold and unfiltered, and he'd gotten it. Only, he'd prefer she keep that *unfilteredness* to his mother's case and not his emotional shortcomings. Some things didn't need to be analyzed.

Hell with it. He walked in.

Jenna and the sheriff stood in the middle of the living room where crime-scene photos were spread in a path to the sofa. A flash of white on one of the photos—his mother's pajama top, the one with the pink hearts—caught his eye. Sickness consumed him and he immediately brought his gaze to Jenna. *Close one.* As usual, that punch to the chest hit him. This time it was more of a kick. A solid boot right to his sternum. This woman tore him up. By the time she got done with him, all that compartmentalizing he'd done since the age of five would be shattered.

But never before had he felt that boot to the chest. There were women he'd enjoyed, in all kinds of ways, but none who did this to him. Was that good or bad?

Psychobabble. That's what it was.

Either way, he wanted her.

She hustled over to him, grabbed his jacket sleeve and angled him away from the photos. "Hi."

"What are you doing?"

He calculated the myriad of ways she could answer and anticipated her putting him off, making up excuses, *avoiding* him.

"I'm not sure."

That, he hadn't expected. "Come again?"

She waved her arms. "I know it sounds crazy, but there's something in the photos that's bugging me. I needed to walk through the house again, get it set up the way it was that night and study it."

"Why didn't you call me?"

"You were mad at me."

Had him on that one. The sheriff cleared his throat. *Thank you.* Brent glanced over the top of Jenna's head. "Sheriff, thanks for coming out."

"Sure thing, Brent." He pointed to the door. "I'll give you a second. Holler when you're ready."

Good plan. They didn't need a cheering section. Brent held the door open and closed it after the sheriff walked through.

Puckering her lips, Jenna eyed him, angling her head one way then the other. "Are you still mad at me?"

"I don't know. But guess what? Apparently there's this thing adults do that's called talking, and we should probably do it."

Suddenly, her face lit up and she burst out laughing. "Talking? You?"

Yeah, me. For a second, he stared at her, but her face revealed a whole lot of nothing. Then he leaned over and kissed her. An easy press that warmed his blood but didn't spark like the last kiss, which could have taken down a city. He backed away and ran the pad of his thumb over her bottom lip. Great lips.

"I want to apologize. About before. At your place."

Still didn't fix the problem, but hopefully she'd recognize the step he'd taken. But was recognizing it enough? She deserved more than some broken-down guy with emotional limitations. Most of the women he'd dated had. He was just never willing to give them what they deserved.

"I accept your apology. Thank you."

"I *am* scared."

Oh, damn. He'd said it. *Strong men don't do this.* Needing her out of his space, he retreated a couple of steps.

After the second step back, Jenna followed him, gripped both of his arms and squeezed. "Look at me."

Slowly, he breathed in and looked down at Jenna, concentrating first on her stormy blue eyes that changed with her moods, and then on those perfect lips.

Was she speaking? Her lips were moving, but it all sounded gibberish.

"Did you hear me?"

He shook his head.

She brought her hands up, cupped his face, and her palms were warm and steady and soft and made him think of things he shouldn't necessarily be thinking. Things involving his bed over a long weekend.

"Can you hear me?"

The fog in his head cleared. He nodded.

"I said I don't blame you. You've been through a trauma no one should experience. Especially not a child. I think you've programmed yourself to constantly self-protect. Maybe I'd do the same thing. But eventually, all this self-protecting will backfire. It might be forty years down the road when you're sitting alone on a holiday because you have no family left, but it'll catch up. And that will be ugly. You can either let people in or you can stay closed off. Personally, I think closed off would be lonely."

He brought her hands down, but not wanting to break the contact—*what am I doing?*—held on. "Before a couple of hours ago, I hadn't thought about it. Right or wrong, I'm doing what I know."

"Maybe you should let people help you so you can know something different."

"People do help me."

She jerked her hands, but not enough to break free. "You know what I mean. You have friends and your family, yes. But outside of that you have no interest in opening yourself up to anything but sexual relationships. If that's how you want your life to be, fine. We'll stay friends or business associates or whatever you want to call it, and that'll be that."

"Is that what you want?"

"It's not, but as much as I think your self-preservation theory is a crock, I'm not about to walk into an affair with a man who will slaughter me."

"Exactly why I wanted to be honest about my priorities. This case is my priority."

Finally, she tugged her hands free. "You're not ready for this. We should stick with our original plan until I'm done on your case."

Was she kidding? He'd just emasculated himself in front of her and she was turning tail? "I'm not sure what you want from me."

"Don't make me slap you. You admitted you were scared and I love that. It's a major step. But we're all scared, fella, and I can't handle you falling back on the excuse that you don't have time for a relationship. Tell me you're scared and leave it there. Don't bulldoze me with this no-time theory."

Frustration burned in his gut. This shouldn't have been this hard. "I don't know what to do with the fear."

"You do nothing with it. You—*we*—take it slow. Nobody says we're getting married. We go out. We—hold on now, don't panic—go on dates. Dinner. The movies. Ball games. If it's a disaster, at least we tried. But hey, that's just me. And, since I'm working your mother's case, you don't have to come up with excuses to break our dates. I'll probably break them before you do."

Slow. She'd said it. Not him. Usually he was the *take-it-slow* one. This woman was destroying all of his excuses. Every last one. Son of a gun. He dug his fingers into his forehead and rubbed. At some point, he'd laugh about this. Right now? *No.*

"What's wrong? I'm blowing your theories to bits?"

He laughed. "Pretty much."

"It's not a bad thing."

"Feels like it."

She smiled at him and then tugged on his shirt. "You're not used to it. Relax."

Had he ever done that? Maybe with the guys watching a game, but with women? Never. Always on guard. Waiting for them to want more of what he couldn't give. And then they'd walk away and he'd be fine—A-okay—with it.

The way he felt right now, if Jenna walked away, he'd tackle her, grab her ankles and beg her to stay. Talk about emasculating.

Man, oh, man, his life suddenly got a whole lot more complicated. "Dating, huh?"

"Yes, Brent, dating. It's a concept I know you have problems with."

He rolled his eyes. "Harsh."

She poked him. "I couldn't resist."

"Next time, try. Rome wasn't built in a day."

That cracked her up enough that she snuggled into him, wrapped her arms around his waist and squeezed. "You're a good guy, Brent Thompson."

When it came to relationships, he wasn't convinced of that. For her sake, he hoped it was true. "When we're done doing whatever it is we're doing at my mom's, do you want to have a late dinner with me?"

"Like a date-dinner?"

"Yes, Jenna. A date. I'm asking you on a date. But if you drive me crazy with this, I'm bailing."

"Wow. I was simply clarifying. I'd love to have dinner with you. Thank you."

Step one complete. And he'd survived. "Perfect. Now what the hell are we doing here?"

WHILE BRENT WAITED on the porch, Jenna collected the crime-scene photos she'd spread across the floor.

"What's next?" Sheriff Barnes asked.

The man had been here two hours and the gravelly tone

in his voice had become more prominent. He'd already worked a full day and she was peppering him with questions, forcing him to recall a murder that happened twenty-three years ago. A murder he hadn't been able to solve.

She stacked the last of the photos from the living room and straightened the pile. "Thank you for doing this."

"It's not a problem. You didn't figure out what was bothering you."

No. She hadn't. *Thanks for the reminder.*

"Not yet. But I will. It's here. I just haven't tripped over it yet."

He gestured to the remaining photos stacked on the floor next to her briefcase. "We haven't been through those yet."

"Those are perimeter shots. Some from the morning after, but most from that night."

"We're here. We might as well do it." He swung back and opened the front door where Brent waited on the porch. "You're good."

A few seconds later, Brent entered the house, his big body filling the vast emptiness. This had been his home, a place he should recall happy things, memories of playing and family gatherings, Christmas mornings and birthdays. What did he see when he stepped in here?

One day she'd ask him. Not now. Getting in touch with his feelings wasn't high on his to-do list, and she'd already gotten a win with him admitting his fears about emotional attachments. She wouldn't push it.

At least not yet.

"We're almost done," she said.

Hands in pockets, his go-to stance when he wasn't sure how he felt about a situation, he cocked his head and squinted at the photos in her hand.

She waved the stack. "These are perimeter shots. It won't take long to go through them."

He nodded. "Did you tell the sheriff about your visit to Jeffries's?"

Sheriff Barnes slid his gaze to Brent, then to Jenna. "What?"

"He called his lawyer." She scrunched her nose, thought about the wasted hours. "We're setting up a time to chat."

"I'm not surprised. We've talked to him enough that he panics when he sees us pull up."

"I thought I hit on something with that hunk of cement from his collectibles."

The sheriff smiled, but it was one of those tight-lipped smiles that stunk of failure. "Nothing doing there."

She shrugged. "I snapped some pictures while he was out of the room. If nothing else, it's something to think about."

Along with the bazillion crime scene photos she'd yet to get through. She'd studied all the interior shots, but only a few of the exterior ones. *Exterior.* Sharp, searing stabs blasted the back of her neck. "Oh, wait."

Brent was already in motion, moving toward her. "What?"

Jenna dropped to her knees and fanned the perimeter shots she held, spreading them across the floor. *Where is it? Where is it?* "Come on. I know you're in here."

Squatting next to her, Brent touched her arm. "What are you looking for?"

"I don't know. Something."

There. A photo of the back entrance taken the night of the murder. She studied the photo. Back door closed, folding chairs on the porch. A baseball bat originally thought to be the murder weapon but ruled out. A football and a baseball sat next to it. Next picture. *Where is it?*

Flicking a couple of photos aside, she scanned two others, taken in sequence and then lined them up next to each other. Together they were a complete view of the house.

The entire area had been lit up, probably by spotlights so the crime scene guys could work the area.

"Jenna?"

"Give me a second, Brent."

Go slow. Study each one. Blood stains on the porch? Displaced items? There had to be something. On the photos, she trailed her finger over the steps, and then to the side of the porch where firewood had been stored in an iron rack. "What about the wood? Was that checked?"

"Every piece of it," the sheriff said. "Clean."

"Dammit."

She moved on. Nothing but grass. Except. Wait. On the ground near the side of the porch, the edge of something peeked out. She went back to the stack of photos, snatched the next two pieces to her puzzle, lined them up and found nothing but more grass leading to the driveway. Whatever peeked out wasn't visible in the other photos. Shoot.

Glancing up at the sheriff, she tapped the photo. "Any idea what this is? Was it taken into evidence?"

The sheriff squatted beside Brent, his gaze darting over the photos and, if Jenna guessed right, his mind racing.

"It was dark," he said. "We went back in the morning to make sure we got everything. Whatever that is, I don't remember it."

Jenna hadn't seen anything on the evidence list that resembled this item. If they had it, she'd know. Brent stood tall and she looked up at him. "Any ideas?"

"Let me see that."

She handed him the photo. He analyzed it for a few seconds, clearly his law enforcement brain organizing thoughts and then, like a bomb had exploded, he dropped the picture and bolted. "I think I know what it is."

Chapter Nine

Brent tore down the porch steps as if he was chasing a loose football. *Get there, get there, get there.*

All these years his father had stored those bricks under the house. For what purpose, Brent never knew and never cared. They weren't bothering him, so he left them there. And maybe he was wishing for it, but whatever was in that photo had the faded reddish color of a brick.

In the pitch black, his breathing coming too fast—*control that*—he dropped to his knees, ripping the lattice off the bottom of the porch and sending a few hunks of wood flying. He closed his eyes. Better not to get a chunk of wood lodged there.

After a few seconds, he opened them and adjusted to the blackness. *Need light.* He pulled out his phone, shined the light from the screen. Not enough.

Jenna leaned over the porch rail. "Brent?"

"Flip that light on. I need a flashlight."

Setting his phone down, he tossed the broken lattice aside and pulled off the remaining pieces. *Ow.* He held his finger over the light. A sliver of wood had pricked his skin. At least it wasn't an eye. He tried to fish it loose, but the sliver broke, leaving half still lodged in his finger. He'd get the rest later.

The porch light came on, throwing shadows across the

trees behind Brent. Jenna came around the house, limping a little on that bad ankle—the crutches were where?— and carrying a giant flashlight that had to belong to the sheriff.

"I think it's a brick," Brent said. "In the photo. There's been a stash of them under the porch for years. I saw them last month when I had to fix the lattice."

A sudden sick feeling jabbed at him, turned his stomach inside out. All these years he'd been chasing leads and the murder weapon could have been sitting under the damned porch. No, couldn't be. All those bricks had been checked twenty-three years ago. Unless someone added to the pile after the fact. He let out a huff because—hell—he didn't know what to feel. Useless came to mind. His face grew hot and his head pounded. *Boom, boom, boom.* A swarm of pain and rage and torment devoured his system. *Coming apart.* He banged his hand against the side of the porch. "It's been under my damned porch all this time."

Jenna stepped closer, set her hand on his shoulder. "Brent, hold on."

No. He jumped to his feet, started pacing, just tearing up the ground, wanting to rip something apart because what kind of an idiot has a murder weapon sitting under a porch for twenty-three years and doesn't know it? Dammit. "Twenty-three years. Unbelievable. After the sheriff's office checked the initial stash, I never counted or bothered to check them again. There could be DNA on that thing! After all this time, who knows if there's anything decent left. How stupid am I?"

Jenna threw her hands up. "You are *not* stupid. I got lucky with that photo. Right place, right time. If I hadn't seen that hunk of cement at Jeffries's house, I may not have even caught this. And without you, we wouldn't know the bricks were under the porch."

The sheriff walked up behind Jenna, stowing his cell. "Sorry. Phone call. What's up?"

"Brent thinks there are bricks under the house. What's in that photo might be the edge of one. I don't remember any bricks on the evidence list so if it is a brick, it was missed at the crime scene."

Brent squatted again and shined the light into the general area where he'd remembered the bricks being. There they were. A dozen or so, stacked in even piles. "They're here. I need to crawl under there."

Think like a US marshal. This could be potential evidence. Evidentiary procedure had to be followed. The chain of custody alone could derail a case. It would take time, but each brick would need to be labeled with details about when it was found and who handled it. "I can't do it."

Barnes nodded. "Damn right you can't. If we find a murder weapon under there, the victim's son shouldn't touch it."

"The defense will have a field day," Jenna said.

All of this, he knew. One slipup and the bricks could be inadmissible. Ideally, they needed the State Police to send a crime scene investigator to handle evidence collection and marking.

But they didn't know if this truly was evidence. For all they knew, they had a stack of worthless bricks.

"I'll do it," Barnes said. "I was part of the original investigation, and if it comes down to it, a prosecutor can make that fly. I'll take it to the lab myself to keep the chain of custody intact."

"Perfect," Jenna said. "We have a private lab the firm uses. It'll be quicker."

That'd cost a fortune. A fortune Brent didn't have. Just as he was about to say it, Jenna turned to him. "The firm will cover the cost. Penny told me that early on."

Next time he saw Penny, he wouldn't tease her about how short she was. He wouldn't tease her about anything. Ever again. Well, that might have been pushing it, but for the next while, he'd leave her alone.

At some point, he'd figure out a way to thank her and make her understand how grateful he was. Suddenly, after all the years of no progress, maybe they'd be able to close his mother's case and give his family closure.

Closure.

He despised that word. Wasn't particularly sure he even understood it. One thing he did understand was that when they found his mother's killer, he'd have to find a way to deal with his messed up emotions. Once the killer was found, his goal would be achieved. And after spending his entire adult life—every spare second of every spare minute of every spare hour—studying his mother's case, he'd have to figure out a way to move on.

Barnes turned back. "Let me get gloves out of the car."

While Barnes chased down gloves, Jenna stepped closer. "Are you okay? You're quiet."

"You could be right about the bricks. The color is right."

"That's not what I'm talking about."

Of course it wasn't. She wanted inside his mind again. Maybe soon he'd let her in. Now? He couldn't do it. That storm of emotions already churned, filling his lungs and trapping his air. When it broke through, it would drown him.

"I know." He touched her face, ran his finger down her cheek and over her jaw, and that simple motion—the connection—centered him. "I can't go there. Part of me wants to. It's…" He shook his head. "It's too much."

There. Best he could do. Lame as it was. He just hoped she understood how difficult lame could be.

She went up on tiptoes and—*hey, now*—kissed him. Quick. Probably didn't even qualify as a kiss, but he wouldn't complain. Not when that minor peck told him that she wouldn't bug him about his emotional failings.

The damned kick to the chest happened again, pounding at him as if he was supposed to do something. Whatever *something* was. But when she backed away, he wrapped his hand around her head and held her there, kissing her the way they'd done it earlier. Fast and hard and making sure his intent was clear. He wanted her and—surprise, surprise—it was about more than sex.

If dealing with his pit of emotional garbage scared him, thinking about a *relationship* might give him a coronary.

The crunch of boots on dry leaves sent Jenna leaping backward, but her gaze was on him and a wicked smile met his.

"We'll finish that later." She spun to Barnes, already shifting to work mode. "We can compare the shape of the bricks to the wou—"

She glanced up at him, brought her fingers to her mouth and tapped. Still, she was protecting him. Noble, but a problem.

"Unfiltered, Jenna."

She dropped her hand. "Wound. If we can match the shape of the wound to one of these bricks, we have the murder weapon."

"And possibly DNA," Barnes added.

Could they get that lucky? Brent didn't think so. This exercise, like all the ones before, could be a bust.

Jenna stepped forward, tugged on his shirt and met his gaze. "It's okay to be hopeful. I'm hopeful."

"I know, but…" He waved his hand. "All the disappointments."

Barnes handed them each two pairs of gloves. "You won't be touching anything, but we all wear them. Double 'em up. No chances."

"Yes, sir."

Barnes dropped to his belly. "Here we go. I'll take photos before I bring anything out."

Overhead, a bird chirped and Brent looked up. Wind rattled the almost barren tree branches. Slowly, he walked to the back end of the house, turned and came back. This could be it. A murder weapon. *Don't go there.* Not yet. But…maybe. Jenna watched him. *No talking.* Please. No talking.

After fourteen laps and some serious mind-shredding later, Brent saw Barnes crawl from under the porch. The sheriff, straightened and brushed moist dirt from his clothing. "I got a broken one."

"Ooh," Jenna said. "Let me see."

Stooping low, he grabbed the broken brick from the pile. "Don't touch it."

"I won't. Let's take it inside." She turned to Brent, making hard eye contact in the dark. "I'll compare it to crime-scene photos."

Translation: *I'm going to look at photos of your mother and don't want you to see.*

He could live with that. Even if the waiting might kill him. Then he wouldn't have to live with anything.

She left him standing beside the house, but he strode to where he could see part of the porch and Jenna just inside the front doorway. She held a photo, the overhead light shining down on her. "What is it?"

"I think we've got something."

"What?"

From her spot, she looked down at him. "I had the sheriff line the brick up with the wound on your mom's head. The corner of the brick looks like a match. We could have our murder weapon."

JENNA OPENED THE outer front door of the building and stared into the dimly lit hallway leading to her apartment. Two hours earlier, they'd found that stash of bricks, all of which were now at the lab. Maria, her scientist friend, didn't appreciate being called on a Sunday evening, but as Jenna often did, she talked her way around it.

Even if she now owed Maria a huge favor.

"Everything okay?" Brent asked from behind her.

After the kiss he'd hit her with earlier? No. Everything was not okay. And now he had to go and be a gentleman and walk her to her door. She was no fool and her no-fool self knew his protective instincts ran deep. After that kiss, there was definitely something else running deep.

On both their parts.

She angled back to him. "What are we doing?"

"I don't know about you, but I'm pretending we didn't make an agreement about the…uh…*physical* aspects of our relationship."

He was no fool either. "We said we'd go slow."

"What's your point?"

She laughed. Then to her great horror, stepped inside, waving him in while her brain and body sent conflicting signals. *Do it, don't do it, do it, don't do it.* Her brain may have known what it wanted, but her body was buzzing in a way she'd only felt…well…never. That's what this was. A first. Firsts didn't happen often and she wasn't exactly one to let an opportunity slide by.

"Don't ask me if I'm sure. I'm not. My brain is saying one thing, but my body is definitely saying another. And I like what I'm hearing."

Brent cracked up and the sound of it—the newness and unexpected pleasure of this tormented man lightening up—filled her. Sure, she'd heard him laugh before, but he'd held back, muffled it under the weight of grief. This laugh came right from his belly, and she'd made it happen.

I'm a goner. "Let's go."

She left the front door open and darn near sprinted to her apartment, glancing back to make sure Brent followed. Yep. There he was, marching toward her, his gaze on her as she reached the door and jammed the key in the lock. Or at least tried to. Wrong key. *Shoot.*

"I'm stupid with lust right now." Again he laughed that amazing belly laugh and—oh, my—she wanted to hear that over and over. "Brent Thompson, if you ever fake laugh in front of me again, there will be hell to pay. That's a promise."

Finally, she shoved open the door, reached back and grabbed his jacket, hauling him inside. The timed lamp on the end table had switched on and threw soft shadows across the room. "You promised me a late dinner, by the way."

"We can order."

And even as he said it, he ditched his jacket and tossed it on the chair by the window where she'd forgotten to close the drapes. Forget it. Her plan didn't include the living room anyway. She slid her jacket off and dropped it. Brent inched closer, sending her body into sizzle land.

"Pizza. Later."

"I like pizza."

"Excellent. Follow me."

Walking the narrow hall to her bedroom, she stripped off her shirt, tossed it back to him and he laughed again. "Is this some twisted stripper act? If so, it's working."

Her bra came next and she threw that back as well. A few more feet and they'd be at her bedroom where he'd see her naked from the waist up. Her body had been judged countless times, from all angles in all sorts of outfits. But that was fifteen pounds ago and never naked. Now that extra fifteen pounds spooled into nervous tension and gripped her. *He said he likes my curves.*

She stepped into her darkened bedroom and stopped. When his arm came around her, she didn't flinch, just settled back against him where his erection poked her lower back. Oh. Boy. He dragged his hand up, gently cupping her breast, and heat shot to her core.

"You're beautiful, Jenna."

In all the times and ways people had told her that, it was never more than words simply coming at her. She'd heard it so much, somewhere along the way, it became meaningless. Except those words never sounded like this. So filled with meaning and…and…truth. When Brent said it, her heart opened up and took it in.

And she believed it.

BRENT COULDN'T STAND IT.

All he wanted was to strip Jenna naked and spend the entire night exploring her lush body. Pure torture. When she went for the button on his jeans, he didn't stop her. He also didn't stop her when she shoved them down to his ankles, letting her fingers skitter over his hips—and other places.

If she'd had any doubt about his level of interest, he'd just blown that away. Far away.

He stepped out of his jeans, kicked them to the side and dealt with the condom from his wallet. He ripped his shirt off and stepped forward, nudging her against the bed until she fell backward and scooted to the center. Needing his hands on her, he grabbed her ankle to hold her still, and then dropped next to her.

Lowering himself on top of her, he took a second to let that skin-to-skin heat absorb. Damn, he loved that. Loved that the woman under him was no beanpole and he didn't have to worry about snapping her in two. He kissed her neck, nipped at her chin and smiled when he coaxed a tiny moan from her.

All these months of picturing her naked and sprawled under him, on top of him, beside him—any way he could get her—and it had finally happened. Yeah, he'd take his time. Not rush to the end and that big bang that cleared his mind. This time, he wanted slow, then fast, then slow again. Endless minutes to memorize every place he touched and kissed and nibbled.

With Jenna, that's all he wanted.

Another moan. *She's mine.*

He buried his face near her ear. "I like that sound. Is that what you do when something feels good?"

Slowly, she slid her fingers along his back and—*whap!*—smacked his butt. "I guess it is because what you're doing feels good. *You* feel good."

He nuzzled her ear, trailed kisses along her jaw, anticipating that first second, the ultimate pinnacle of his fantasy when he entered her. Months of thinking about that moment, and here it was. Waiting for him.

Jenna arched against him, prodding him to make a move. To do *something*.

"You don't have to get pushy about it," he said.

"You're teasing me."

"I'm enjoying you. Big difference."

And something he hadn't done in a long time.

"Enjoy me later."

Certain things in life had become clear in the past few days. Jenna being brutally honest was the first. The second was he hadn't laughed enough. Until Jenna, he hadn't laughed nearly enough.

He kissed her again, lingering a second while she hooked her legs around him. He pushed and—*oh, man*—the shock of those first few seconds of being inside her made him gasp. He dropped his head, breathed in and she arched against him, urging him on. Locking her legs, she held on while they moved together in that first-time rhythm that would—if he had any luck—move to second- and third-time rhythm.

Another moan, this one louder, came from Jenna and he moved faster, wanting to hear it again and again and again. So close. He was so close to that edge and hanging on, just ready to go over, but for once not wanting it to end.

Damn, he'd turned into a sissy. *Who cares?* When it came to Jenna, he didn't care.

Her body bucked and she arched up, gasping and—*zap*—his mind fried. He looked down at her, took it all in. The way her mouth tilted up, her long hair spread across the pillow, her closed eyes—*beautiful*—and his world came apart.

Sprawled on top of her, his breaths came out short and shallow. Cripes. He needed to pull himself together. Get control of his mind and body because—hell-to-the-yeah—every Jenna fantasy he'd ever had needed to be explored. Every damn one of them. And he'd do it. Slowly.

She ran her hands over his back in a sweeping motion that if she kept up he'd drop to a dead sleep. "That feels good," he said.

"*You* feel good. I knew you would. Knew it."

"Good," he said. "Because I love you."

Chapter Ten

He *loved* her? He did *not* just say that. Not now, when things had been so perfect. So fun. But no, Brent had to remind her just how emotionally twisted he really was.

As much as she'd fooled herself into thinking they could have a fling, a physical release that would satisfy both their curiosities, she should have known better. She cared too much. About him. About his family. About his mother.

Now he claimed he loved her, and she was just needy enough—and smitten enough—to believe it and get her heart stomped on when his infatuation cooled.

Brent rolled off her, his big body landing precariously on the edge of her queen-size bed. *Need a bigger bed.* Great. Already buying king-size furniture for the king-size man she had no business buying anything for. With his need to close himself off and her need for constant approval, they'd be New Orleans the day after Katrina. One heck of a mess.

But she had yet to respond to his big announcement. What was a girl supposed to do with that? *Thank you? Back at ya?* No.

He rolled to his side, kissed her bare shoulder. "I promised you pizza. I'm starving."

Pizza. Really? She shook her head, smacked her palm against her temple and shook again. Yep. Fully awake. "Um, did I miss something?"

"I said I'm hungry."

"Before that. The thing you said."

He cocked his head, closed one eye. Thinking. *He must be joking.* How could he forget something that important?

"The I-love-you thing," she said. "Did I hear that right?"

Brent laughed and in one quick move was on his feet, dealing with the damned condom and collecting his clothes, all those yummy muscles and hard lines of his body kicking up her pulse.

"You heard it. We don't have to talk about it."

Oh, now she got it. People said all kinds of nutty things during an orgasmic high—not that she'd ever been afflicted with that particular problem. But obviously, Brent had.

And now he needed to backpedal because he was afraid she'd start dropping the "L" word also. *That* made total sense. A weird sense of relief set in and the sudden tension in her shoulders eased.

"It's all right. I just didn't know what I should do."

Brent zipped his jeans, checked that all was in proper order and shoved his T-shirt over his head. "About the fact that I love you? Or that I said it?"

"Uh…both?"

Again, he laughed. "You're funny. You don't need to do anything. I said it. I meant it and we can be done."

"You can take it back."

He gave her an *are-you-on-medication?* look. "Is this third grade? Why would I take it back?"

She grunted—*take a second*—and rolled to the opposite side of the bed where her bathrobe hung from a hook on the wall.

"You know what I mean. We were caught up. It was fun. A great stress reliever. Even if you think you're in love, you're probably not."

Propping his hands on his hips, he stared up at the ceiling and blew air before facing her again. Everything about him, the stiff stance, the squinty eyes, the locked jaw, screamed impatience. Well, excuse her for wanting to clarify. Any woman would.

"Jenna, I know you were a psychology major, but last I checked I know how I feel. I may stink at sharing it, but I know. And I sure as hell don't need you telling me. Thanks for that, though. I'll be in the living room."

Darn it. Knotting the belt on her robe, she followed him down the hallway, his long strides fast and purposeful. Mad again. Too bad. He would not goad her into a fight so he could deflect the subject. No chance. *Snap.* Her brain clicked into gear. How had she not realized that when he didn't like a topic, he picked a fight? The best defense is a good offense. Brilliant.

"Brent, that's not what I meant and you know it."

He stopped, just halted in his spot and stared straight ahead. "What did you mean, then?"

She scooted by and swung to face him. "I was giving you the out, in case you didn't mean it. You just sprung this on me after great sex. What was I supposed to think?"

"You weren't supposed to think I was lying about it. You're the one always on me about talking, so I talked. What, in your experiences with me, makes you think I casually throw that phrase around?"

Big fella had her there. She opened her mouth, thought for a second, got nothing and blew raspberries.

"Okay, well, can we hit the reset button here? I was surprised. And confused. I didn't mean for it to become war."

He squeezed his eyes closed, scrunched his face and dug his hands into his hair. "I'm horrible at this. I've had this…I don't know…thing…for you. For months now. Every time I see you I get this crazy feeling in my chest. I've never had that before. Maybe I got caught up in the moment or whatever, but I don't say things I don't mean."

She waited, desperately hoping some revelation would

hit her. Nope. Nothing. But the panic was there, shooting up her arms and into her neck, making her face hot because she'd had a thing for him, too. Since that first day she'd seen him in Penny's office, they'd simply *clicked*.

Wait. She couldn't do this. Couldn't let herself believe he actually loved her. If she believed it, she'd start to want things. Things like the two of them sharing meals and secrets, grocery shopping, lazy Sunday mornings. A backyard with a swing set. The two of them making a life together.

Worse, she could *feel* it. Those little moments when he smiled at her or teased her. That settled feeling she got when he touched her. All of them firsts. Firsts she hadn't wanted to read too much into.

Until he told her he loved her.

"You don't have to say anything, Jenna. I don't expect that." He shrugged. "Let's see where it goes."

Oh, this had to be a trap she was about to step in. It couldn't be that simple. "I feel it, too. Whatever that something is. I'm not ready to say it, though. It's too important, and when I say it I want to know, without a doubt, what it means."

"It's okay."

"Well, this is crazy. Usually I'm the one needing the positive reinforcement."

He snorted. "Well, it's new territory for me, too. I need to get used to it. Maybe enjoy a relationship for a change. Can we do that?"

Relationships, even good ones, were never easy. Throw in a man with repressed feelings and a needy ex-beauty queen and it might be the worst combo ever. But what if it weren't? What if, in some backward way, they balanced each other?

That might be the biggest and most welcome surprise of her life.

Brent waved a hand in front of her eyes. "Have I turned you to stone? You're not saying anything."

"Yes. We can do that. It will require you to feed me, though."

She reached for the phone, but he brought her into his arms and kissed her. Nothing crazy and definitely lacking the intense heat they'd shared earlier, but these soft, gentle pecks promised more. These were the kisses of coming home at night, leaving in the morning, rushing to do an errand. Those wonderful and comforting everyday kisses she sorely missed.

She backed away, setting her hand on his cheek. "I thought you were starving."

"I am. Just thought it was important to wait on it a sec." He grinned. "Now order my damned pizza, woman."

"That'll be the day."

Still, she ordered the pizza. The extra-extra large. Just in case. She set the phone on the side table, and then glanced at the front windows and the open drapes. Perfect. At street level, in her bathrobe, groping a man. Great show for the neighbors.

She moved closer, grabbed one of the drapes to flick it closed and—*crash*! She spun toward the window and all at once her mistakes hit her. *Other way. Turn. Now.* She swung her head to the right and covered her eyes, protecting them from the prickling shards of flying glass. Something hard and heavy bounced off her shoulder and skidded across her jaw, ripping at the skin before thunking to the floor. Memories of her brothers' teasing—*protect your face, beauty queen*—roared back. *Not-my-face, not-my-face, not-my-face.*

She staggered for a second, her head looping and spinning. Sudden warmth seeped down her cheek. *Please, no blood. What if it's blood? No blood.*

She brought her gaze to Brent, shook her head wildly because—dammit—her life had been spent primping, playing up her looks, using them to get ahead and...*I'm bleeding*. Pathetic, pathetic Jenna. Nausea consumed her and she held her arms out. *Hold on. Hold on.*

"Jenna!"

Brent's voice. Eyes shut, she focused, listened for any sound other than his voice. No shattering glass, no thunking objects, nothing. Safety. She opened her eyes as Brent lunged for her, reaching for his gun while watching the window.

Liquid warmth trickled over her jaw and she lifted her hand.

"Don't," he said. "You're bleeding."

Her face. Bleeding. *How bad, how bad, how bad?* Her looks were everything. Her first foot in any door, her ultimate weapon and now, if the seeping blood was any indication, she had a gash down the side of her face. One that might scar.

Scars meant her mother would stand in front of her, checking every inch of that gash. Normally, she'd beam. *Oh, look how beautiful you are. Perfection.* What would her mother see now? Now she'd mourn perfection. She'd see the marring and the pain would be too much.

"Are you okay?" Brent asked.

Was she? No way to know. "Yes. Go."

He charged for the door. "Call 9-1-1 and lock this door after me."

She nodded, her head bobbing like some dumb waif. "Be careful."

Great. She'd just told a US marshal to be careful. Suddenly, she was his caretaker? He'd *love* that. Not that it mattered because she'd just been hit by—what?—she glanced at the floor and there it was, of all things, a brick.

BRENT HAD HAD ENOUGH. Whatever Jenna thought about that was too damned bad because she was done. Off this case. Now maybe she'd be convinced the gas-line incident wasn't a fluke.

After checking the perimeter around Jenna's house, he hustled down the short hallway leading to her flat and rapped on the door. "It's me. Brent."

The door swung open and there she was, still in her silky bathrobe, holding a washrag to her bleeding cheek. He checked her feet. She'd thrown on his sneakers, probably because they were the closest to her and she didn't want to step in glass. The way he'd torn out of the house, he may have a shard or two in his feet, but right now enough adrenaline flooded his system to numb any pain.

"I called 9-1-1," she said. "Police are on the way. Did you see anything?"

"By the time I got out there, they were gone."

She pointed. "It was a brick."

"I saw it."

And hadn't that been a life-shortening experience? Standing there as all those shards, like airborne ice picks, flew at her. And the brick. That one freaked him out good. His pulse hammered and he locked his teeth together. A few inches higher and that brick would have clocked her on the temple.

"Brent, don't go there."

He straightened up, met her snappy gaze. "Someone just threw a brick at you. You could have gotten your head bashed in."

And he'd stood there watching, half-frozen.

"But I didn't."

Sirens drew closer—cops. Any second they'd come storming in and see Jenna in a thigh skimming, silky bathrobe that now hung open at the neckline to reveal a substantial portion of her mind-blowing chest. Distracting himself from his own imagination and thoughts of her dead on the living room floor, he waggled his hand.

"Uh, you might want to put clothes on."

She glanced down, gasped and kicked out of his shoes. "I'll just throw something on."

"Yeah. And I need to look at that cut. You may need a couple of stitches."

If they were lucky, that would be the worst of it. This time.

No. There'd be no next time. Whatever argument she'd hit him with, he'd be ready. One thing was for damn sure. He was pulling Jenna off this case.

Two hours later, Jenna sat on an ER gurney waiting for the doc to stitch up the gash on her cheek while Brent leaned against the wall, stewing. Every inch of him burned. Continuous blood from Jenna's face combined with the closed-in, putrid hospital odor didn't help his foul mood.

"Brent, you look fierce."

"Maybe because someone just tried to kill you. Or do you think that was a random act, too?"

"Oh, my God, please tell me you're not picking a fight with me after someone just trashed my house."

He paddled his hand in her general direction. "I wouldn't have to pick a fight if I thought you'd be reasonable."

"How was I supposed to know someone would toss a brick through my window? And, if you'd relax, you'd realize someone is upset, which means we're making progress."

Unbelievable. As much as he wanted to rip into her, he'd remain calm. *Calm.* "Do you not get that someone just hurt you?"

With her free hand, she pointed to her cheek. "Trust me, I get it. Not only was my home violated, but I have to sit here and get my face, my ultimate tool, stitched up. So, don't tell me I don't get it. I assure you, I'm feeling everything I'm supposed to."

Great. Finally. Common sense. "Then we won't have any problems. I'll take you to my place or to your folks or wherever, but you're not going home. By the way, your landlord is boarding up the window for you."

She jerked her head. "Already?"

"Yeah. Your neighbor came over to check on you when you were with the cops. I gave her my cell number. She texted me a few minutes ago and said the landlord was there. Your place is secure, but I'm not taking you back there."

"So, that's it?"

Not in this lifetime did he think Jenna was giving in this easily. "Pretty much."

"You're going to tell me where I can go and when. Are you going to change my diapers too?"

If he were in a better mood he'd laugh. "I'll do whatever it takes to keep you breathing, Jenna. Including taking you off this case."

Still holding the bandage to her cheek, she hopped off the gurney, marched over to him and squared off. "Don't you dare. You cannot take this from me."

He stared at the wall behind her, focused on the sign explaining patients' rights. If he looked at her, he'd probably find those baby-blues pleading, working him like she worked every other man with a pulse.

"I can and I will."

"Look at me."

He glanced down, then away again. As good as she'd get.

"Fine. Don't look at me, but on a purely professional level, if this were anyone else, you wouldn't do this. If I were a man, you wouldn't do this. If we hadn't slept together, you wouldn't do this."

"I'm not going to argue that."

"Damn you!"

Finally, he looked into those firing blue eyes that should have peeled flesh off him. *Settle her down.* He reached for her, but she snapped her arm away.

"Hey, I refuse to let you wind up dead. Simple as that. Be mad at me if you want because, in this case, I don't care."

"You are so stubborn."

Again, he wouldn't argue. She stomped back to the gurney, hopped up and pulled the bandage from her face to check it.

"Still bleeding," he said. Precisely why he'd talk to Penny and pull her off this case. "This is too dangerous now. It's no coincidence you got hit with a brick."

"You're firing me because I got hit with a brick?"

Simple as that. "Yes. I'll take it from here."

"Oh, of course you will. You get my help in making progress and now you want to shove me aside."

"No, I want to keep you alive."

Outside the room voices erupted, something about a GSW—gunshot wound—and Brent figured they'd be waiting awhile yet.

Time to fix this. This time, he'd go for the softer approach and hope that her level of fatigue would get her to back off. He wandered over to her. "Honey, listen to me."

"Don't *honey* me." She poked him—hard—right in the chest. "You." Another poke. "Can't." Poke. "Do this to me."

Yes, he could. He wouldn't stress that. With the look on her face, he might be the next gunshot victim here. "Jenna—"

"Please," she said, her voice tight and strangled, life dripping out of it. "Please, don't do this to me. I haven't craved a lot of things professionally. Joining the FBI was the only thing, and I fell short. After that, it's been tiny victories. Little milestones. Until your mom's case." She focused on him, those blue eyes not nearly as hard. "I need to see this one through, Brent. Please."

I'm burned. Done. He dropped his shoulders and stared down at the floor. Option one: give in and let her finish

this. Option two: don't give in and have her never speak
to him again.

Option two stunk.

It would also keep her alive.

Gotta do it. He faced Jenna again, took in her sad eyes
and knew this would hurt.

"I handled that wrong. I'm sorry. I'm worried about you.
And you getting hurt was not part of this assignment." He
tugged on the ends of her wild hair, then swept the long
strands back over her shoulder. "I want you in one piece.
That's all."

"I know. And I love that about you. But I need this."

"I'm sorry, Jenna. I'll call Penny and have her go to your
place. Pack you a bag. Or I can do it. Not sure you want me
rifling through your stuff, though."

The curtain flew open and Penny and Russ stepped in.
Jenna leaned back and Brent dropped his hands. Penny's
laser-sharp gaze whipped between the two of them. For
once, considering it was ten o'clock at night, she wasn't
wearing one of her power suits. For this trip to the ER she'd
dressed down in slacks, a crisp white shirt and heels. Russ
stood behind her in jeans and a sweatshirt.

"I heard my name," Penny said.

Jenna threw up her hands, revealing that still-bleeding
cut on her face. "Really, Brent?"

"Hey," he said, "she's your boss and your assignment
put you in danger. You can bet I called her."

Penny marched over to Jenna and inspected the cut.
"Jenna, that's nasty."

"Gee, Pen, thanks."

"Sorry."

"She needs stitches. They've got a GSW down the hall.
Guessing we'll be a while."

"Penny," Jenna said, "he's going to try and talk you into

booting me from this case. I'm telling you right now, I won't be happy if that happens."

Brent drew air through his nose before his mind left him and he started yelling.

Women. Always hassling him. His phone rang—*thank you*—and he dug into his pocket. "I'm taking this. It'll give us a second to cool off."

On his way out of the room, he gave Russ the *shoot-me-now* look.

If he got her out of here and she was still talking to him, much less having any interest in pursuing their personal relationship, it would be a minor miracle.

Barring that miracle, at least she'd be alive. He'd be okay with that.

Even if Jenna wasn't.

THE SECOND BRENT stepped into the hallway, Jenna went to work on Penny.

"He's freaking out because I got a brick through my window. You and I both know I've been in much more dangerous situations than this. We know it. I can take care of myself. All this incident means is we're getting close to something we're not supposed to get close to. The fact that it was a brick can't be ignored. I've scared someone, possibly the killer and when people are scared, they make mistakes. Mistakes that leave evidence to convict them." She looked at Russ over Penny's shoulder. "Tell her."

Russ held up his hands. So much for him helping.

She went back to Penny. "Please. Don't pull me off of this. I'll take precautions. I'll make sure I always have someone with me. I'll even stay with my folks. Well, maybe not them because my dad will freak, but I'll find somewhere safe to stay. Please, Penny. I need this."

Penny stared right into her eyes. Assessing. Good. If she'd already made up her mind, she would have said so. Hesitation from her boss might be the opening Jenna needed. One she could exploit.

"Give me another week. Earlier tonight we dropped a brick off at the lab. I think it's the murder weapon. It's unlikely we'll get prints off of it, but DNA is possible and maybe we'll have our murderer."

"Nice work, Jenna," Russ said.

"We found it under the porch at Brent's mom's. The sheriff came with us to keep the chain of custody intact."

Russ moved closer. "That's why you got a brick through your window."

But Jenna kept her focus on Penny, who continued to stare at her. "Yes. I can handle this. Please. Tell him I can handle this."

Apparently, that was all her boss needed. Penny turned to Russ and he gave her the all-purpose *eh* face. *Distract them*.

"And, Russ," Jenna said, "I'd planned on calling you earlier. Can you help me track down Brent's father? I tried the number Brent gave me, but it belongs to someone else now. I could dig around, but it'll be faster if you do it."

"Now you want the big man mad at me, too?"

"Sorry."

"What about the junkie?" Penny asked.

Now they were back to Jeffries. Jenna was fairly certain he was a dead end.

"I'm not ruling him out yet. I need to talk to Brent's father and see how I feel about him. Then I can start focusing on one or the other. If we get DNA off that brick, we might have a slam dunk, but that might take a few days, and I don't want to lose momentum."

Brent stepped back into the room and they all shut up.

"Suddenly everyone gets quiet." He glanced from Jenna to Penny and then to Russ. "What momentum?"

For whatever reason, Jenna didn't want to talk about this

in front of him. Call it survival, call it protective instincts, call it whatever, but she didn't think he needed every detail. He'd said himself that he couldn't wrap his mind around his father hurting his mother. "We're talking about the brick."

"Huh, I'm sunk now if even Russ is quiet. No way I'll win against all three of you. Even if I am the client and want you off this case."

"Brent," Penny began. "You *are* the client here. I'll do whatever you want, but your goal in this was to heat up the case. Obviously, you and Jenna have done that."

No kidding there. As if he'd read her mind, Brent slid his gaze to Jenna and their eyes held for a long moment while her mind flashed back a few hours to her bedroom and how they'd made each other smile.

No one was smiling now.

Brent gave in first and turned to Penny. "I'm worried about her."

"I know. I worry about her all the time. But this is her job, and if she wants to see this through, it should be her choice."

"And what if something happens to her?"

"We'll make sure it doesn't."

Brent scoffed, shook his head, then scratched the back of his neck. Killing time. She had him. Time to move in.

"Please, Brent," Jenna said. "I'll be careful."

His eyes were on her again, growing darker by the second, and she held her breath. The tension between them ran so thick an ax couldn't penetrate it, but she sat tall, challenging him. He wanted her to give in. To crumble. To let him have his way. Well, she wouldn't. Not this time.

Being the smart woman she was, Penny swung to Jenna and then back to Brent before turning to Russ. "Am I missing something here?"

"What are you asking *me* for?"

"You had a beer with him earlier. Maybe you know something."

"He doesn't," Brent said.

Jenna didn't believe it any more than Penny did, but that was between Russ and Brent. If Brent had shared his thoughts about his relationship with Jenna, good for him. At least he was talking to *someone*.

Even if it did sting a little bit that she wasn't that person. *Later.* There'd be time to worry about that later, when she and Brent actually figured out what the hell they were doing with each other. Aside from having multiple orgasms.

Jenna puffed up her cheeks, felt the tug of skin on her still-seeping wound and winced.

Brent moved to the bed, got right into her space. "You can't go home. We find you somewhere else to stay and you don't go anywhere alone. Whatever we have to do, I don't care. You can't be alone. Those are my terms. You agree to them and you stay. If you argue, you're fired."

At once, her toes, her fingers, her arms, everything tingled. *Yes!* Victory. He wouldn't see it that way, and she definitely wouldn't point it out, but she had most definitely won this round. Maybe there was hope for them yet, because stubborn Brent Thompson hadn't sacrificed her. He could have, but he hadn't.

Penny rolled out her bottom lip and studied the two of them for a few seconds. "I don't know what's going on and I'm not sure I want to, but, Brent, if you need to be somewhere, I can drive Jenna wherever she needs to go."

"I'm good," he said. "I'll make sure she's safe."

Penny clucked her tongue. "I'm sure you will." She spun to Russ. "Russell, shall we go?"

Oh, boy. She'd busted out the *Russell* business. Poor Russ would get a grilling in the car. Any other time, Jenna would have jumped in and asked to speak to Penny alone. To tell her that Russ was an innocent in this mess and even if Brent had confided in him about their relationship—or whatever the subject was—Penny should leave him alone. But, as confused and tired as Jenna was, she didn't have it in her tonight.

Even if she did, she wasn't sure what she'd say to Penny. *Hey, boss, you know how I'm not supposed to get up-close-and-personal with clients? Well, Brent is amazing in bed. In case you were wondering.*

Before Penny and Russ could leave, shoes squeaked from outside the room and a female doctor, who looked about twelve, stepped in. "Sorry for the wait, folks. Let's get this problem fixed up."

Jenna didn't want to be a whining patient, but this was her face. One she'd have to see in mirrors for the rest of her life, and a twelve-year-old wanted to stitch her up? The doctor shoved her hands into gloves and smacked open a cabinet where she messed with items, ripping open packages, fussing with gauze. Little by little, panic climbed in Jenna's throat. She knew nothing about this doctor, and the woman was about to shove a needle into her face. Her no-fail, always-come-through-for-her face.

She's going to make me look like Frankenstein's monster.

Brent moved to the side of the bed, hands propped on hips. "You okay?"

No. She shot another look at the doctor, and then came back to him.

And then, as if something clicked, Brent nodded. "Uh, doc?"

The doctor set supplies on the tray near the bed and turned, her gaze shifting to the butt of Brent's sidearm that stuck out from the hem of his shirt. "Is that a weapon?"

He dug into his pocket for his wallet and badged her. "Brent Thompson. I'm a US marshal."

"I see. Did you have a question for me?"

"I do. No disrespect here, but are you by any chance a plastic surgeon?"

Thank you. Jenna hadn't said one word, but he knew.

The doctor glanced at her and Jenna turned her face, putting the vertical gash on display.

"No, sir, I'm not. But I can stitch up a wound."

"I don't doubt that and, again, no disrespect here." He tucked his finger under Jenna's chin and inched it up. "But look at this face. Tell me you can stitch it up and it'll be as perfect as it was before she got cut."

About to follow Russ out the door, Penny took it all in and Jenna dared no eye contact. Her boss wasn't stupid and Brent jumping into the fray, putting his hands on Jenna in such an intimate way was sure to have her perception-radar blinking.

The doctor studied the gash again. "I can't guarantee that. A plastic surgeon couldn't, either."

Brent nodded. "I understand and appreciate your opinion, but we'll take our chances with the surgeon."

"Sir—"

"I want the surgeon," Jenna said. "I'm sorry, but you're a woman. Please understand."

Voices erupted from the hallway. "Coding!" someone shouted.

Snapping off her gloves, the doctor tossed them in the trash and spun to the door. "I have to go. I'll see who's here."

"Thank you," Jenna called.

Penny smacked her hands together. "Okay. Well, that was…interesting. You're in good hands here, so Russ and I are leaving. Call me in the morning. We'll talk. Count on it."

Chapter Eleven

First thing Monday morning, Jenna hunkered down in the Hennings & Solomon boardroom with a whiteboard, the box of files she'd made Brent retrieve from her apartment and all of her notes.

Avoiding the bazillion questions that would come from her family, she'd opted to spend the night in a hotel. Plus, if she knew anything about her boss, Penny would ask, in no uncertain terms, where Jenna had slept the previous night and Jenna wouldn't have to lie. She wanted to truthfully tell Penny she'd slept in a bed alone.

Of course, Brent had insisted on playing bodyguard and slept on the hotel room's sofa, which was rather heartbreaking since he was twice as big as the thing and couldn't have gotten any decent sleep. But there were only so many battles she could win with him, and, as tough as she'd played it, his presence calmed her. It let her feel a little less wary.

None of that could be admitted. All that would do was ignite the argument that she should walk away from his mom's case. Instead, they'd found a compromise with Brent following her to work and escorting her upstairs after which he went off to make sure a federal witness got to the court-house unscathed. Right now, that witness—bless him—got

Brent out of her space so she could make sense of her notes without her personal feelings interfering.

Penny popped her head in the door. "Good morning, sunshine."

"Hi."

"How's the face? I'm assuming the big, bad marshal got you a plastic surgeon?"

Jenna turned her head, revealing the bandage running from her jaw to midcheek. "Yes. He did. Eleven stitches."

Penny rolled out her bottom lip and narrowed her eyes in the way she did when focusing on a potential witness. "That was something, seeing Brent take over like that. He has a protective nature about him though, so I'm not sure why I was surprised."

Anytime now, Penny would find a way to pry about what she'd witnessed at the hospital. "He's a good man."

"He is indeed. Where did you sleep last night?"

Good old Penny. "I was too tired to deal with my family so I went to a hotel. Got the highest floor and double locked the door."

"Uh-huh."

"What?"

"Are you lying?"

"Nope. Want to see my receipt?"

Penny circled one finger in Jenna's direction. "You better not be lying."

"I'm not. Promise. Why would I lie?"

"Because Russ has gone into Band of Brothers mode and clammed up. That tells me Brent told him something, and he's refusing to betray his confidence. I love that about Russ, but when he uses it against me, I could stab him and dump his body."

Jenna cracked up. Penny, all five-foot-one of her, didn't pull any punches. "Thanks for the laugh. I needed that."

"Tell me not to worry about whatever is going on with you and Brent. This is business, Jenna, but he's my friend and I care about him."

"You don't have to worry. We're fine. We're both adults and we know what's at stake. I promise you. We're fine."

After a solid thirty seconds of silence, Penny waved her off, then gestured to the papers spread on the table. "What's this?"

"I'm working on a murder board."

"Ooh, can I help?"

As a defense lawyer, the most morbid things excited Penny. Jenna supposed the constantly thickening skin came with the job.

"Sure. I'm adding suspects to the white board. It helps me sort everything."

Penny grabbed a marker out of the fancy oak pencil box on the credenza. "You tell me what to write."

"I have this Jeffries guy and Brent's father. The sheriff is double-checking on any home invasions in the surrounding areas around that time. So far he's come up with one person. The guy was nineteen at the time and didn't have a history of violence. He was a petty thief looking for jewelry and small items to hock."

"Where is he now?"

"Lives in Indiana. His name is Carlton Boines. He did a two-year prison stint the year after Brent's mom died."

Penny made notes on the board as Jenna babbled. "Here's a photo of him." She handed Penny the picture and tape.

"That could be something. What else?"

For the next thirty minutes, Penny made notes on the board. By the time they were done, they had a lineup with three photos. Boines, Jeffries and Brent's father. That was it. Three suspects. Not a lot, but a start.

Jenna shoved her notepad away and sat back. "While

we're waiting for DNA on the brick, I'll find Boines and then start working on family members and acquaintances of his and Jeffries. Anything from Russ on Brent's father?"

"That's what I came in here for." She held up a note. "Russ got you this number and an address in Severville. It's near the Kentucky state line."

How interesting that Brent's father lived just over seven hours south and hadn't taken the time to let his children know. "Thank you. I'll call him."

"How does Brent feel about you questioning his father?"

Jenna set the note on the table. "He hasn't said. Not a shock since he doesn't say much about anything."

"You've read the evidence, what do you think? Did Mason kill his wife?"

"Penny, I honestly don't know. He's still considered a suspect. They just don't have any solid evidence. But after meeting Jeffries and finding out the sheriff doesn't have diddly on him, I have to start looking elsewhere. And that means questioning Brent's other family members about the relationship between Brent's mother and father."

"Did they get along?"

Jenna scrunched her nose. Somehow it felt like a betrayal sharing what Brent had told her, but this was Penny. His friend. Someone he trusted. "He said they yelled. Plenty of couples yell and it's not abusive. It's simply the way they communicate. Brent may have been too young to know the difference."

Still holding the marker, Penny tapped it on the table. "And you're afraid of what you'll find."

"And I'm afraid of what I'll find. From what I've gathered, Brent's dad doesn't have it in him to kill someone. He's weak. Evidenced by his walking out on his children. But we've seen crazier."

"We sure have. You have to question him. If nothing

else, to rule him out." Penny leaned forward and spun the phone toward Jenna. "Let's call him."

Yes. Let's. She eyeballed the number, grabbed the phone and dialed.

By the third ring, her hopes were dying fast. *Come on, be there.* Voice mail. Drat. Maybe she should just drive down and surprise him? Always an option. A long beep sounded and Jenna left a generic message telling Brent's father her name and that she was calling from Hennings & Solomon. That was it. If nothing else, he'd be curious why someone from a law firm would call him.

She dropped the receiver into the cradle and pushed the phone back to its original spot. "Now we wait. I'll talk to Brent's cousin. His aunt isn't comfortable talking about her sister. At all. She gets that deer-in-the-headlight look every time I'm around. Plus, Brent adores her and I don't want him annoyed if I push too hard. Jamie and her father are easier to get information out of."

"It's like walking through a minefield."

"Let me tell you, my psychology degree is coming in handy. I could do a thesis on this family. They were all questioned and apparently ruled out years ago, but they're still traumatized and no one wants to admit it. Instead, they stare at an empty house and watch Brent drive himself crazy. Tragic. Any way you slice it."

Penny checked the clock on the wall. "I have a client call in five minutes. Mike will go with you to track down Boines. Don't go alone."

For once, Jenna wouldn't argue about taking her rival, a retired detective and Hennings & Solomon's other investigator, with her. The itchy stitches on her face were all the convincing she needed. The irony of her marred face was not lost on her, because suddenly the beauty queen couldn't use her looks to get information out of men.

This she'd have to do on skill alone.

THERE WERE PLENTY of things about this case that bugged Jenna, and sneaking off to Carlisle without telling Brent might be the one that bugged her most. Even if she'd planned on telling him—after the fact—she was defying his request that she inform him when contacting his family. Plus, her goal today was to garner information about his father, about whom he clearly had conflicting emotions.

But he wanted his mother's killer caught, and that meant poking around in his parents' marriage.

The only thing she knew for sure was that she despised the knot of fear stuck in her throat. Someone had put a brick through her window and whoever that someone was, they didn't want her poking anything. Well, too bad. The stitches on her face alone were enough to push her forward. If she had a scar, when she found the person who did this to her, she'd beat them senseless.

So, with time ticking and Brent working, she'd recruited Mike to play chaperone. She also brought along her .38 for added protection.

Jenna exited the tollway with the midmorning sun shining through her windshield. Great day. Days like this weren't made for fear. They were made for strolling the lakefront, snuggling up with a sweetie, holding hands. All the good stuff. Maybe at some point, she and Brent would do that. Was he even the strolling type? So much to learn.

She let out a small sigh and hooked a right into the truck stop where Jamie had agreed to meet her. Wanting to keep this meeting out of eagle-eye Aunt Sylvie's range, Jenna had concocted some nonsense about a time crunch and asked Jamie to meet her at the truck stop to save her thirty minutes of driving.

The entire thing might be a joke because these people were so tight that Jamie probably had hung up with Jenna and called her mother. Still, if they met at the house, Sylvie would be all up in their business and calling Brent wanting to know what was going on. And considering Brent didn't know, well, enough said.

Complicated. Not so much the professional aspects, but the emotional ones. On a professional level, she had no problem going rogue and hunting down witnesses. Brent was different. The double orgasm the night before proved that. Now she'd slept with him, gotten emotionally involved and—*voilà!*—immediately began hiding things. How would that look to him?

If the roles were reversed, she'd think she was being used.

Which he would despise. And couldn't be further from the truth. For a second, she considered calling him, just admitting the whole damned thing. For a second. Then the investigator in her grabbed hold and smacked her upside the head. This was her job. Emotions must be removed. That meant Brent and her feelings for him, that comfort she felt when around him, the way her body responded when his big hands touched her skin, all needed to be set aside.

"Jenna Hayward, cliché of the year," she muttered. "That's me."

"What?" Mike asked.

"Nothing. Talking to myself. You can wait in the car. I don't want to spook her. Just keep an eye out, okay?"

"Sure."

She parked and glanced around the parking lot. To her right, a few truck drivers stood gabbing in front of their rigs. The fuel pumps were relatively quiet with only two cars in need of their service. No Jamie. Jenna checked the time on her phone. Five minutes early. She'd wait. Maybe grab a cup of coffee from inside.

But that meant walking around with this hideous bandage on display. She flipped the visor mirror open, fluffed her hair a bit, pulling it forward. Nice try. Even with long hair, the bandage was visible.

Eh, who needed coffee?

She'd just wait. Maybe answer some emails. Call her family. File her nails. Anything to not think about Brent and the multiple orgasms.

Heck of a mess. *He'll be steamed at you now.*

Out of the corner of her eye, she glimpsed Jamie's Jeep pull up. Perfect. No more stewing about Brent. She grabbed her purse and hopped out. Jamie did the same, but Jenna was hoping they could talk in her car.

"Hi," Jamie called. "Who's that with you?"

"Just a coworker. We have a meeting after this."

Total lie, but it would do.

"Ah. It's a beautiful morning. How about we get coffee and sit at one of the picnic tables?"

Coffee and an outside table. *Terrific.*

"Great," Jenna said, finger-brushing her hair forward.

Jamie came around the front of the car, moved in to give Jenna a hug and stopped.

Yep. Here we go.

"What *happened*?"

"Just a cut."

"How on earth?"

How much to tell her? Obviously, Brent hadn't shared last night's drama with his family, and Jenna wasn't sure it was her place to do so. On any other case, she wouldn't even consider talking about it. In her mind, it fell under the rule of privileged information. But Jamie was a friend, right?

Sort of.

Again with the emotional entanglements. Friendships had no place in an investigation.

Jenna waved it away. "I'll tell you about it later."

They marched by the truckers, a couple of guys in their forties wearing jeans, ripped T-shirts and filthy baseball caps.

"Hey, ladies," one of them said.

"Morning," Jenna chirped.

Wait for it.

"What's your hurry?" the bigger guy cracked. "Come over here and let us have a look at you."

Jenna grabbed Jamie's elbow. "No, thanks. You boys have a great day."

"You could make it better," the other one yelled.

She sure could. By showing them her .38. Idiots. Jenna sighed. "Keep walking. They won't bother us."

"You get that a lot, huh?"

Sure do. Sometimes, when it served a purpose, she encouraged it. At least she used to before she had the blasted ugly stitches. "If being objectified by men is the worst of my problems, I can handle it."

Inside the truck stop, they bought coffee and Jamie added a donut—this family loved their sweets. Jenna paid for the items, keeping her head partially cocked so her hair would feather over the bandage. What was she doing? People stared at her all the time. Why did this have to be different?

This time your face is a mess.

That's why.

Hurrying out of the shop, Jenna led Jamie to a group of picnic tables near the grassy area. She glanced to her right and noted the truckers saddling up. Good. What she didn't want was them wandering over and harassing them.

Jamie dove into her donut while Jenna creamed her java and then retrieved her notepad. That donut looked pretty good. Had to be five hundred calories. Had to be. She loved a donut every once in a while and the proof of that was in the fifteen pound weight gain since her pageant days.

"So what's up?" Jamie set down the donut and licked frosting off her thumb.

Go to work. "I mentioned on the phone I have questions about your uncle Mason."

Jamie flicked her glance to the donut, then came back to Jenna. "Did Brent say it's okay?"

Something in Jamie's tone, that squirrelly hesitation, sparked a nerve. Jamie had something to say and it wasn't necessarily good.

"I haven't told him yet. I wasn't sure how to handle it, and I don't want to upset him. But he wanted me to investigate and that means digging into his parents' marriage. No way around that. If you're concerned about it, I can keep this conversation between us. As much as I can anyway."

Because if Mason Thompson was a murderer and went to trial, they'd probably all be called to testify.

Jamie winced. "I hate talking about his family without him knowing it. It feels like a betrayal and I love him. I don't want him hurt anymore."

I know how you feel. All too well. Brent and his brooding, nontalking self had wormed his way into her life, and she wasn't letting him go. It might devastate her, because men like Brent were tough. They had those steel exteriors that wouldn't let people in.

And she wanted in.

Jenna reached across the table and squeezed Jamie's hand. "If it helps at all, I know how you feel. I probably shouldn't admit this, but I'm pretty crazy about him myself."

"I knew it. When he went searching for you at dinner the other night, I could see it. Plus, he's anxious when he's around you. With the way he's acting, he could be a male dog waiting on a female in heat."

Only half-horrified, Jenna snorted. "I'm definitely not telling him you said that." She drew her hand back, picked up her pen. "I just wanted you to know I won't hurt him.

Whatever you tell me, I'll protect him. As much as I can, anyway. I promise."

Jamie squared her shoulders. "Okay. Ask me your questions."

"Thank you. Can you give me an idea of what Brent's parents' marriage was like? Did they fight a lot? Were they happy?"

"All parents fight."

"So, nothing crazy. No domestic violence?"

Jamie stayed quiet, her big green eyes on Jenna, but not necessarily sharp or focused. *Mind wandering.* "I never saw him hit her."

Hit her. Quite specific. *Too* specific. And Jamie was still staring in that strange way that begged to be questioned. "I feel like you want to say something." More silence. *Move on.* "Brent's father worked evenings, right? Was that ever an issue?"

"Not that I know of, but he didn't like people at the house when he wasn't there."

From inside her purse, Jenna's phone chirped. Bad timing. She ignored it. "Like who?"

"Female friends were fine, but no men. If they needed work done on the house and repairmen had to come, he had to be there."

"Was there a reason? Did he have trust issues?"

Sure sounded like a jealous husband. In Jenna's line of work, she saw a lot of that.

"I don't know. Maybe. I overheard my mother complaining about it one night. Mason didn't like my dad going over there when he wasn't home. My mom was appalled. It wasn't like they were having an affair or anything."

Oh, hey, now. *That's fascinating.* Jenna set her pen down hoping the lack of note taking might loosen Jamie's lips more. "Do you know if there was a history of adultery? Either of them?"

"Heck, no."

"You seem pretty sure."

"Well, I...huh."

"What?"

She shrugged. "I guess I don't know. I mean who really knows what goes on in a marriage?"

Indeed. "So nothing comes to mind?"

"No. Aside from him not wanting men in the house. That was always a big deal."

"Who were her male friends?"

"You think she was having an affair?"

Here, Jenna needed to be careful. This was Brent's mother, his protective aunt's sister. One slipup and Sylvie would be on Brent about it and Jenna's life would get a dose of misery.

"I don't think anything. I'm trying to get an idea of what the marriage was like."

"I've never heard any rumors about an affair. I think I would know."

"With affairs, it could be a love triangle gone bad. Sometimes the boyfriend wants the woman to leave her family and when she refuses, he gets angry."

"Like I said, I think I'd have heard about that, but if you want a list of the men they were friends with, it's easy. Just look at the phone listings for Carlisle. Everyone knew everyone. And Aunt Cheryl was loved."

Jenna nodded. This trip couldn't be considered a success, but this jealousy thing might be a lead. Brent, in his eternal I-refuse-to-talk mode hadn't mentioned his father having control issues.

"I think that's all I need. If you think of anything else, would you call me?"

"Sure."

Jenna rose from the bench, grabbed her still-full coffee cup, the contents now cold, and tossed it in the garbage can.

"Jenna?"

"Yes?"

"He yelled a lot. Mason."

Ah, this was what Jamie had held back. "What did he yell about?"

"I don't know. Stupid things. If the house wasn't spotless, a dirty dish in the sink, whatever. When it was warm out and the windows were open, we'd hear him. I never saw bruises on her or anything, though. I don't think he hit her."

Jenna set her hand on Jamie's arm and squeezed. "Not hitting doesn't mean he wasn't an abuser."

"I know. He just liked things a certain way and he'd get mad if they weren't."

"I see."

Controlling husband, men not allowed in the house, a lot of yelling. Sure sounded like an abuser. *Dammit.* Part of Brent, the part that had witnessed the yelling and control issues, probably could believe his father was a murderer.

When they reached Jenna's car, she turned to Jamie. "Thank you. I know this was hard."

"I don't want to be starting rumors is all."

"You're not. I need the puzzle pieces and you've helped. Thank you."

After saying goodbye, Jenna slid into her car, waited for Jamie to pull away and, without a word to Mike, retrieved her phone from her purse. One missed call. She clicked on it and the number she'd dialed earlier from the conference room popped up.

Brent's father had returned her call.

Chapter Twelve

"Sometimes I wonder if I'm speaking a foreign language," Brent said.

He stood in the doorway of the executive conference room at Hennings & Solomon trying—really trying—not to lose it on Jenna. She spun from writing something on a whiteboard plastered with photos of Jeffries, another guy and...his father. Her list of suspects. A sick feeling settled in Brent's gut.

Marker still in hand, she scrunched her face, clearly insulted by his tone. She didn't like it? He could give her a list of things he didn't like.

Starting with her going back on her word.

She capped the marker and tossed it into a box on the cabinet beside her. "If that's your greeting, maybe you should try again. And you can start by closing that door so half the office doesn't hear you."

Right. Mad as he was, making her bosses an audience wouldn't help her career. He stepped in, smacked the door shut and crossed his arms.

"Oh, you're definitely about to pick a fight."

Ya think? But no, he wasn't owning this one. *This* one fell squarely on her. "Actually, you started this one."

"Me?"

But the way she looked at him, a little pouty and

innocent, wasn't jibing. He eyeballed her, shook his head at her dramatics and walked to within a couple of feet of her. Jenna held his gaze, her body unmoving, but in all that stillness, they both knew she was busted.

"Brent—"

"I had two requests." He held up a finger. "That you not go anywhere alone." The next finger. "And that you give me a heads up when talking to my family."

"Right. I didn't go alone, but I did talk to Jamie."

"At least you're honest about it."

"I can explain."

"Terrific."

She rolled her eyes. "I hate it when you're a jerk."

"And you don't think you were a jerk today? Sneaking off to talk to Jamie?"

Her shoulders dipped forward, deflating like one of those giant air balloons he saw in front of stores having blow-out sales.

"If I was, then I was a jerk doing my job."

This is where he had to be careful. When she hit him with those sparkly blue eyes, his system went wacky, and if he didn't keep that in check, she'd talk her way around him.

"I don't understand why you kept this from me."

"Because I wasn't sure what she'd tell me. I wanted her to feel like she could talk to me without hesitation. I'm fairly stunned she told you. She seemed concerned that you'd be upset."

"She didn't tell me."

"Well, she was the only one there."

Having spent even a minimal amount of time around his family, she should have anticipated how this worked. Instead, she chose not to give him a heads-up and left him blindsided. Something he hated above all else.

"Jamie told my aunt and, guess what, babe? I had *her*

all over my butt. Getting hysterical because we're digging up skeletons."

"Then maybe you should be having this conversation with Jamie, because she's the one who opened her mouth."

"How about we get back to the fact that you lied to me?"

Jenna bunched her fists at him. "I didn't lie to you."

"Lying and lying by omission are the same."

Bottom line: he'd trusted her and she'd blown it. The one time in his life he'd given in, let down his guard and—*whomp*—he got burned.

Coming closer, she held out her hands. "No, Brent, they're not."

He didn't care. Why should he? If he couldn't trust her, what was the point? "I need to be able to trust you."

"You *can* trust me."

Her eyes were so big and blue a man could lose himself in those suckers. Dive right in and never come out. He should walk now. Get it over with and maybe they could stay friendly when they saw each other.

Except she latched on to his arm, the beauty queen with an iron grip. "Whatever you're thinking, we will talk this through."

No talking. Talking was the hell that burned inside him. If he let that out, game over. He'd never recover. Fighting his urge to bolt and leave this nonsense, the emotional chaos and stress behind, he locked his knees.

"Tell me I can trust you."

Where'd that come from?

She moved closer, and squeezed his arm. "Yes, you can trust me. I wasn't trying to hurt you. On a personal level, I'm protecting you. Part of that means not telling you things. If there's something you should know, I'll tell you. Otherwise, let me do my job."

One at a time, she uncurled her fingers. Maybe in case he tried to bolt. To test his theory, he flinched and she latched on again. Despite himself, he half-smiled. Somewhere in this mess, her holding him hostage was funny.

He patted her hand. "I'm not going anywhere."

Still, she hung on. "You can trust me. Please know that."

He tilted his head, ran his finger along the edge of the bandage on her cheek. All because of his mother's case. He'd put her in danger, unintentional as it was. He'd gotten her into this.

"I'm usually the one in charge," he said. "Everyone comes to me for answers. When my aunt called me, I didn't have any and I felt…weak."

"Feeling weak doesn't make you less of a man. It makes you human. If you don't have answers, maybe I do. Give me that chance. Ask me before you get mad. That's the only way this will work. Your family is great, but they know how to work you. I told Jamie you didn't know we were talking."

"And she turned around and told my aunt."

Jenna touched her finger to her nose. "Jamie didn't want to be the one to spill the beans on me so she went to your aunt. Why she did that, I don't know."

"She probably felt guilty keeping it from me." He shook his head. "She stinks at secrets."

"Whatever her reasons, she pitted us against each other and we can't have that. Professionally or personally." She twisted his shirt in her fist and tugged. "I need you on my side. Can you do that?"

He turned it over in his mind, stretched it in all directions. Instinctively he knew the answer, but communicating it didn't come so easy. Being on her side meant being on no one else's. That steadfast, unconditional acceptance. He'd never had that with anyone outside of his sister and his aunt's family.

Time to try it.

He nodded. "I can do that."

She went up on tiptoes and hit him with a lip-lock. Right

there in the conference room where anyone could walk in. He dipped his head lower, skimmed his hands over her waist and settled them in that groove at the base of her back. The tips of his fingers skimmed her butt and his chest went crazy again. Damn, he loved that.

Loved her.

He backed away, nibbled her bottom lip. "Where are you sleeping tonight?"

"Hopefully wherever you are."

"I think we can make that happen."

THE FOLLOWING EVENING, after depositing his witness at a safe house, Brent checked his dashboard clock. 6:30 p.m. Early. Any other night, he'd hit the gym and grab a bite. Plus, it was the first of the month, a time he usually made the rounds of his law enforcement friends asking for any and all updates on cases similar to his mom's.

Tonight, he didn't have it in him. For the first time, even more than chasing down his mother's killer, he wanted to go home to someone.

Specifically, to Jenna. After a life spent numbing himself to emotional attachments, a high-maintenance ex-beauty queen suddenly made him want to mix things up. He rested his head back and his stomach rumbled. Dinner first, gym later. But that didn't sound like a banner evening. He checked the clock again. 6:32 p.m.

When he'd called Jenna earlier, she'd said she'd be at her parents' for dinner until eight. Where she was sleeping tonight, she hadn't said. She'd spent last night with him and he was definitely hoping for a replay. All Brent knew was he hadn't seen her since that morning and didn't like it.

He grabbed his phone from the cup holder and shot her a text.

SLEEPOVER?

No one would ever call him a romantic with that line. Eh, he'd find other ways to please her.

The text buzzed back.

PENNY WOULD CALL YOU A PIG.

No doubt. And it made him laugh as he typed.

I MISS YOU.

Come on. First I announce I love her and now this. Definitely losing my man card.

But what the hell? He pushed send.

Seconds later came her reply.

OMG! LOOK AT YOU ADMITTING YOUR FEELINGS. I'M SO PROUD. I MISS YOU TOO. SLEEPOVER=YES

"Score," he whispered, grinning like an idiot.

His phone buzzed again.

WINDOW AT MY PLACE IS FIXED. I NEED CLOTHES. MY BROTHER WILL DRIVE. MEET ME THERE.

She was sticking to her word of not traveling alone. Finally, they were in sync.

In many ways.

He responded to her text, telling her that he'd pick her up and they could go to his place. He lived in a high-rise with better security.

Plus, he wanted her in his space again. To give it life and energy rather than it being the place where he spent hours studying homicide cases. He dragged his hand over his face, and then rubbed it over his chest where that damned Jenna explosion wouldn't let up. He had a woman in his life and it wasn't just about sex and the release that came with it. Sex for the sake of sex never hurt, but this was different. Now, he wanted her around. A lot.

"Yeah, dude. Things are changing."

Whatever. All this thinking wouldn't solve his problems. For now, he'd take it as it came and hope like hell they found a killer.

At 8:25 p.m. on the dot, he buzzed Jenna's apartment. Seconds later she swung open the door. "We have to go."

"Where?"

She stepped around him, hobbling on that bum ankle.

"Are you limping? Where are the crutches?"

"It just hurts. We have to go."

There went his plan for the evening. "Uh, where?"

"Carlisle."

"Now?"

He had yet to move so she latched on to him, dragging him out the door. "Yes, I just heard from my friend at the lab. She sent the report to the sheriff. Now move so I can lock this door."

In the world of law enforcement, getting a forensics report back in forty-eight hours took a minor miracle. Or some serious butt kissing. "How? It's only been forty-eight hours."

"Welcome to the world of private labs, Marshal Thompson."

Gnarly, paralyzing tension rocketed into his neck. For years he'd been chasing leads on his mom's case, and in a matter of days Jenna had uncovered possible evidence and gotten a forensics report. A damned forensics report. He should be thrilled. Or at least hopeful.

What the hell was wrong with him?

Jenna locked the door and turned to him, all blue eyes and a not-so-tight T-shirt. She held up her hands and kept her gaze glued to him. "I can see you're freaking. That's normal. It's been years and suddenly we have movement and you don't know what to think. There's nothing to think. Let's see what the report says."

Made sense. But Brent's feet were cemented to the floor. *Get going.* He should have been sprinting to his car, but nope. Standing stock-still like a pansy.

"Brent?"

"I'm…" He dragged his hand over his face. "I don't know." *Tired.*

Jenna stepped back, tipped her head up to look at him. "You're scared."

Yes. "No."

"You're afraid your mother's blood and your dad's DNA will be on that brick. I don't blame you. But if we don't get there, we'll never know. Whatever that brick tells us has been there for twenty-three years. The only difference between yesterday and today is that we'll know."

That was a good way to look at it. He took that in, considered it. "If my father's DNA is there, I'll lose my damned mind. I'm still hacked that he bolted on us. He's always been a suspect, but I don't go there."

She grabbed his hands and squeezed. "I know. So how about I do it for you? I'll go to Carlisle and meet with the sheriff."

Did he want that? He'd always been the one funneling appropriate information to his family and—yeah—that job stunk. But he had to do it. His mother deserved it and he wasn't willing to let her case die. Not ever.

But someone else being the funnel for a change, giving his tired brain a rest, he could get behind. "You can't go alone."

"I'll be fine."

"No. I'll go with you. I'll sit outside while you look at the report. Then you tell me. Good or bad, you tell me. You good with that?"

"Are *you* okay with that?"

He nodded. "I am. For once, I'm okay not being in charge."

BRENT HELD THE door to the sheriff's office open for Jenna, but she stopped and hit him with those crystal blue eyes that—*whap!*—hit him square in the chest. How the hell did she do that? Even the ugly bandage couldn't smother how gorgeous she was.

"I feel like I should say something," she said.

"Nothing to say. After twenty-three years, I'm about to find out if my father used a brick to kill my mother."

Jenna winced. "It could be nothing."

"Or it could be something. Which we won't know unless you get your beautiful behind in the damn building."

She shook her head, but laughed. "Remind me later to show you how much I appreciate the man you are."

"Oh, honey," he said. "Way to distract me."

"Is it working?"

"Yep." He smacked her on the rear. "Now go."

The sheriff came out of his office, spotted them standing in the doorway and waved. "Hey, gang."

Jenna strode through the small reception area, her low heels clicking on the linoleum. He inhaled the musty smell of a building vacant of fresh air and realized certain things never changed. The institutional feel of the sheriff's office was one of them. This time, though, he had Jenna with him, and he could study the fit of her jeans and the lack of a short skirt. Couple that with the looser fitting shirt and Jenna had made changes in her wardrobe.

Brent shook hands with Barnes. "Sheriff, thanks for seeing us so late."

It had been twenty-three years of gut-shredding for him, as well. It wouldn't be a shock if he'd already looked at the report.

"I have the report in my office."

Brent took a step and Jenna grasped his arm. "You wanted to wait outside."

Right. He had to get used to this. "Yeah. Sorry."

"Don't apologize. If you've changed your mind, it's fine. I want us to be on the same page, though."

"Something wrong?" the sheriff asked.

Brent patted Jenna's hand and backed away. "No, sir. Jenna will take this one. I'll wait out here."

The sheriff's eyebrows hitched up. "That's…different."

"Yeah, it is."

Into the office they went, closing the door behind them. The next few minutes would be torture, and it wouldn't end when Jenna came out, because after this, whatever the news, he'd have to have a conversation with his aunt. He dropped into one of the cheap waiting-room chairs that had been there for ten years. The cushion sagged under his weight, reminding him just how sick of this place he was.

He slid down, rested his head against the top curve of the chair and closed his eyes. *Mom, I hope this is something.* Failure wouldn't do. He had to get this done.

Eyes closed, he waited, listening for the squeak of hinges when the office door opened. He counted to sixty and when he got there, he did it again. On his fifth cycle, the door finally squeaked and he popped to his feet.

Jenna stuck her head out. "Come in."

Their eyes met and held while he walked, but she wasn't giving him any clues. Nada. Then he remembered she spent her days around liars and lawyers and there you go.

"Have a seat," the sheriff said.

Brent leaned against the door frame, folded his arms, and then let them drop. "I'll stand."

"The short of it is that your mom's DNA was found on the brick," the sheriff said.

They had a murder weapon. Brent's breathing hitched and he straightened, set his shoulder blades. "What else?"

"Nothing. No other identifiable DNA."

His father's DNA wasn't on there.

"So," Jenna said, "we have a murder weapon, but nothing else that will help us identify the killer."

Chapter Thirteen

Didn't that make Jenna crazy? Damned DNA. Everyone talked about how great it was. Well, yeah, but not when you didn't have any. The reality was DNA only broke a case a fraction of the time, and this case wouldn't be included in that fraction.

Brent was leaning against the door frame, his shoulders back, his gaze steady, taking this news like the solid man he was.

"I'm so sorry," Jenna said.

"For what? You found the murder weapon. We hadn't done that in all these years. Add this to the brick that went through your window and someone is scared."

"Whoever it is, we have to catch him before he takes off on us."

Barnes rocked back in his chair. "What's this about a brick?"

"Someone tossed a brick through her window the other night. No coincidence."

He tapped his cheek. "Is that what the bandage is?"

"Yes," Jenna said. "I needed stitches."

Hopefully it won't scar. And once again, she was thinking like a beauty queen. No. Not like a beauty queen. Like a woman who didn't want an ugly scar on her face.

"Well, shoot. I'm sorry about that."

"Don't be. As Brent said, we're getting closer."

Brent boosted himself off the door frame and took a step closer. "What's next?"

Needing to move, Jenna stood. "I think Russ can help." Barnes didn't know Russ, though, so this might take convincing. "He's FBI and he's good. I'd like to see if there were any other similar cases around that time."

Barnes pulled a face. "Like a serial killer?"

"I don't know. I'm looking for anything."

Silence ensued while Barnes mulled it over. He'd been agreeable all this time; she couldn't imagine him not wanting FBI help. "Sheriff?"

He finally nodded. "If you think it'll help."

"I do. I'll talk to him."

Another thing she'd be dragging Russ in on. Which, after the fight about meeting with Jamie, reminded Jenna that she needed to bring Brent into the loop that she'd called his father. In this situation, she hoped to travel to Mason Thompson rather than him returning home and causing more upheaval.

Jenna tugged on the hem of her shirt and smoothed it. "We should go. Sheriff, thank you. I'm sorry the brick didn't pan out."

"We have a murder weapon. I'm satisfied."

Well, she wasn't.

Outside, Jenna leaned on the porch rail and breathed in the cool evening air. Building lights illuminated the walkway, breaking up the blackness just beyond. Had she been alone, the creep factor might be too much. But the quiet soothed her busy mind.

Brent rested against the opposite rail and crossed his legs at the ankles. "I wanted more."

"Me, too."

"At the same time, I was terrified my father's DNA would be on that thing."

This is it. Time to tell him about his father. "I know you were. This has to be incredibly difficult."

He shrugged.

"I need to tell you something."

Immediately, his shoulders flew back. "Uh-oh."

"No uh-oh. You asked me to keep you informed. That's what I'm doing. The number you gave me for your dad didn't work. I asked Russ to help me and he gave me a number for your dad in southern Illinois. We're playing phone tag and have exchanged voice mails. I was waiting until I talked to him to tell you, but this seems like the right time."

"This came out of your conversation with Jamie?"

No-win situation. If she said yes, Brent would want to know what his cousin had said. Regardless of Jenna craving a little payback when it came to Jamie's loose lips, Brent didn't deserve to hear nasty things about his father.

"We've known he's been a suspect and I'm talking to everyone, right? Fresh eyes and all that. I just need to talk to him. Then we can rule him out."

"Or not."

Jenna chose not to respond. Cases could go either way and predictions were often wildly incorrect. "When I speak to him, I'll let you know."

He grinned. "So I don't yell at you again?"

"Yes, so you don't yell at me again." She levered off the porch rail, walked the few feet to him and grabbed a handful of his shirt. Her knuckles skimmed his rock-hard abs. *He must kill himself in the gym.* "I don't ever want that to happen again."

He glanced down at his mangled shirt and puckered his lips. "Getting a little rough for someone who needs a place to stay tonight."

"I can always sleep in my own bed."

"Not a chance. Besides, I've got a great bed."

"I know you do."

He tugged his shirt free and slipped his arm over her shoulders. "Then let's go home."

AFTER ANOTHER NIGHT with the incredibly irresistible Jenna—he could use more of that in his life—Brent spent the early part of his morning dealing with the processing of a federal fugitive. He strode through the lobby of the Chicago US Marshals' district office and headed for the stairs that would take him to the fifth floor. The morning rush had dwindled, leaving the cavernous lobby with less than a dozen visitors and employees coming or going. As he approached Lenny, the guard at the reception desk, Brent tossed him a small bag of Aunt Sylvie's cookies. Like Brent, the guy had a thing for the killer salty-sweet combo of chocolate chips and macadamia nuts.

"You're a good man," Lenny said.

"Remember that when I run out of my own stash and raid yours."

Brent's phone rang and before he got to the stairs he ducked to the side to check it. Speaking of the devil. He hit the button. "Hey, Aunt Sylvie."

"Where are you?" The rough-edged tone she used when something had hit the fan immediately put him on edge.

"Just walking into my office. What's up?"

"He's back."

A woman wandered by, giving Brent a long look as she passed. Thanks, but no thanks—that was the last thing he wanted. "Who?"

"Your father. He just showed up."

It took a solid ten seconds to absorb the words, but Brent's body finally stiffened and his ears whooshed. *Concentrate*. He gripped the phone tighter and squeezed his eyes shut. The whooshing stopped and the lobby sounds—dinging elevator, the swish of the revolving door, clicking heels on marble—came into sharper focus. "Wait. What happened?"

"He's here. Right next door walking around like he owns the place."

Jenna was so dead. Just last night she'd assured him that she'd warn him if she'd made contact. "He does own it."

And didn't that stick in his craw considering Brent had been paying the taxes and other expenses on the place since his father had bolted.

"What's he doing here?"

Excellent question. "I don't know. Did you talk to him?"

"Of course not," she huffed. "I saw a strange truck in the driveway and sent your uncle over. He came back looking as if hell had swallowed him and told me the truck was Mason's."

Already, Brent was checking his watch, figuring how long it would take him to tell his boss he had an emergency, get someone to cover transporting his witness this afternoon and get to Carlisle. "Is he still there?"

"No. He and your uncle had words and he left. He told Herb he wanted to see the old place. Good Lord, what if he's staying? I can't do that, Brent. I just can't."

Already with the hysterics. "He's not staying. Trust me on that. Did he leave a number?"

"No, but he asked for yours and your uncle gave it to him."

Good. Let him call. "Okay. I'll clear my day and head out there. If he comes back, stay away from him. Don't upset yourself anymore."

He clicked off and sucked huge gulps of stale lobby air into his lungs. Damned Jenna. She had to have spoken to his father. Why else would he be here? Again she had blindsided him. The woman made him insane. Every step forward, she snatched him back. How many times would she go rogue on him, and how many times would he allow her to talk him out of being angry?

Out of walking away.

And if she thought she was going to give him any BS about wanting to tell him in person, he didn't want to hear it. No chance. The elevator dinged and the doors slid open—hell with the stairs. He'd go upstairs, clear his schedule and then hunt Jenna down.

Within the hour, Brent strode through Hennings & Solomon's fancy waiting area to the desk where Marcie, the young receptionist, greeted him. After his stint on Penny's protection detail last spring, Marcie readily recognized him.

"Please hold," she said into her headset. She connected her call and hit Brent with one of her cheery smiles. "Hello, Marshal Thompson."

Not feeling too cheery, the best he could summon was a nod. Damned Jenna, aggravating him. "Hey, Marcie. Jenna around?"

"One moment."

Marcie located Jenna and directed him back. The Queen of Blindside stood in the hallway outside the bullpen looking nothing short of fantastic in a black skirt and not-so-clingy sweater, and that stupid punch to the chest walloped him. No time for that when his mission right now might include killing her.

She unleashed one of her beauty queen smiles. "Well, hey there. This is a surprise."

It sure is. His steady, direct approach must have been a clue to his mood because her smile melted like snow on a ninety-degree day. "Conference room. We need to *talk*."

"Um, sure." She scooted up to him, balancing on her high heels while he burned treads in the carpet. "What's wrong?"

He ducked into the conference room Penny had used

months earlier to escape from him—her protection detail. Great choice considering his already irritated status.

Jenna followed behind, closed the door and immediately reached for him. *No touching.* Hands up, he halted her. "After everything we've talked about, you blindsided me again."

Her head snapped back. "I'm sorry?"

Not an apology, but a question. As if she misunderstood his meaning. He stepped closer, refusing to let those blue eyes distract him. Not this time. "Let me clarify. I asked you one simple thing and that was to keep me in the loop when you spoke to my family."

"Yes. And I have."

"My father doesn't count? You didn't think it was wise to tell me he was coming here today?"

"What are you *talking* about? He's coming here tomorrow. Not today."

And there it was. She knew and she didn't tell him. "You talked to him and you didn't tell me?"

"I was about to call you."

"You didn't think that was important enough to disrupt my day?"

"Brent, I spoke to him barely thirty minutes ago and then Penny called me into her office. That's where I was when Marcie paged me. As far as your dad, he said he'd be here tomorrow. I was going to call you when I finished with Penny."

Brent figured he must have been from some other planet because he thought it was pretty damned clear he wanted to hear this stuff ASAP. Penny was a reasonable boss. She wouldn't have minded Jenna taking a minute to call him. What didn't she get about that? "He just planted his tail at the house. My uncle talked to him and my aunt is having a damned stroke."

"And that's my fault?"

"Wanting you to call me the second you hung up with him isn't a lot to ask."

She stepped closer, reaching for him, but he backed away, shrugging loose of her hold. Her bottom lip wobbled and she swallowed a couple of times as her blue eyes filled. Jenna crying. That was new. As much as he hated the sight, he couldn't help her. She'd blindsided him for the last time.

"Brent, please, he told me he'd be here tomorrow. Not today. He must have come up here and *then* called me. He lied to me."

"Why would he come here before he even spoke to you?"

"He lived in Carlisle for years, maybe he's still in contact with someone who knows I'm poking around. I don't know, but I didn't talk to him until thirty minutes ago."

Brent jammed his hands into his hair, dug his fingers into his scalp. Blood barreled into his skull, pushing, pushing, pushing until his eyes throbbed from the pressure. Insanity. That's what he had here. All of these people yapping at him and he didn't know what was truth versus fiction.

"My aunt is hysterical. They all come to me. Every damned issue becomes mine to fix." He breathed deep. "I asked you to do one thing. Just give me a flipping heads-up so I can manage the spin. How was that not clear?"

"It was clear. But I don't control what your father does. How was I supposed to know he'd show up today instead of tomorrow?"

"You couldn't, but again, a heads-up about the conversation would have helped. Now I'm stuck with chaos and hysteria. I don't even know where the hell he is right now. He could be on his way to Camille's. I've gotta get over there and tell her before she finds out and goes nuts. That thirty minutes you waited would do me a whole lot of good right now."

"This is not my fault!"

The conference room door flew open and Brent swung

back to find Penny in the doorway, her lips pressed tight. "Whatever you're fighting about, take it down a notch." She scooted in and closed the door. "What's going on?"

"Nothing," Jenna said.

"Doesn't sound like nothing."

"My father showed up," Brent said. "I didn't know."

Penny whirled on Jenna. "You didn't *tell* him?"

And now Penny knew. Brent bit down, waited for his teeth to scream from the agony of all this pent-up anger and hurt and…and…rage. "*You* knew?"

"No, no, no," Jenna said. "She only knew because she called me into her office. I swear to you. She's the only one who knows. I wouldn't do that to you. Brent, I know what you're doing. Please, don't do this."

But Brent was beyond that. To hell with it. All this emotional upheaval surrounded Jenna. She made him crazy. No matter how much he cared—and constantly craved her lush body—he didn't have the stamina for this. He needed calm and quiet. Jenna didn't provide calm and quiet. She was excitement and lust and attachment. All things for him to obsess about, and he had enough to obsess about. *Time to go.*

Turning his back on Jenna, he faced Penny. "I'm concerned for her safety. Great job finding leads, but we've got a killer unhappy with her. I'm pulling the plug. You're fired."

There. Done. Enough said. Without looking at Jenna, he walked out.

FIRED? FIRED. The word left Jenna more than a little dumbstruck. He'd actually done it. Later, when she got over this mind-frying anger, that loss would tear right into her chest and drill through her heart. At this moment, chasing him down the hallway, she was too incensed to feel the pain.

"You are not firing me." She made sure to keep her voice

low, but loud enough that a retreating Brent would hear. "We will take this outside, but we're not done."

"We're done."

They stepped into the elevator and Brent smacked the button, ignoring her. Of course he was. Because if he looked at her, she'd see all his terror carving him up, eating away at him like acid on skin, and God help him if he showed any weakness. Instead, he picked a fight and here they were back at the beginning.

"Putting aside our personal involvement, are you going to jeopardize my career by firing me?"

"I told Penny my reasons. I *told* her you did a good job. If there's any fallout I'll fix it, but I can't do this with you anymore."

So stubborn. All these years he'd been trying to find his mother's killer. Finally, some progress was made and he wanted to end it. He'd have his life back and be able to heal, and he wanted to stop?

Wait.

She looked up at him, the man who pretended to ignore her by staring at the elevator doors. *Locked up tight.* As usual. Because this was his MO. To stay distant and unattached so he could focus on his mother. Avoid emotional conflicts with women. *I'm so dumb.*

"Now I get it."

Finally, he glanced at her. "What?"

The elevator hummed and Jenna glanced up at the flicking numbers. Five, four, three—she hit the stop button and the alarm sounded, a loud, blaring that rammed her eardrums.

"Brilliant," Brent said, reaching for the button.

"Don't touch that button."

He stopped, grunted and turned to her. "I'm not doing this. I'm done."

"Of course you are. Because you're terrified of solving this case. Without it, you'll have to find a way to deal with the emotions you've packed into yourself. You've said yourself you're a bomb waiting to go off. Without your mother's murder, you'll have nothing but that bomb. So, instead, you'll push me away, like you've done every other woman in your life, and then you'll be alone and miserable. Which, oddly enough, seems to be your comfort zone." She flung her arms. *"Bravo!"*

In that annoying way of his, Brent snorted. "Here we go with the psychological evaluation again."

He turned back to the closed doors, focused on them as if they were the most fascinating thing he'd witnessed. *Locked up tight.* This would get her nowhere. That thick skull of his would not be penetrated until he calmed down. She'd have to wait. She hit the button again and the alarm stopped. The elevator jerked and began its descent. Two, one. The doors slid open and he stepped off.

"Don't do this, Brent. Let's chalk it up to an argument, a misunderstanding, whatever, but don't fall back on being a jerk because it's easy. You're better than that."

He paused and a woman, someone from the fourth floor Jenna had seen before, angled around him. Given the late morning hour, the lobby was quiet. At least she'd gotten one break. She waited for Brent to turn around. Waited for him to admit that terror had consumed him. Waited for him to apologize.

A full twenty seconds passed and nothing. Not a word. Just this big, hulking man standing with his back to her. In that deepest part of her where she'd grown to admire him, to care for him—no, to *love* him—that stung. Finally, Brent took a step, hesitated, but no, kept moving, his strides long and fast and heading straight for the door. Away from her.

Jenna didn't move. Maybe, after she'd spoken to his dad, she should have called him on the spot or rushed to wherever he was. Her mistake. One she'd never make again, but she'd thought she'd had time. Simple as that.

She'd thought she had time.

Apparently not.

Well, she did now and Brent had just announced he didn't know where his father was. She'd find Mason. Fired or not, she'd find him. What she did on her own time was her business, and she suddenly felt ill. Not actually a lie since her stomach flip-flopped like an Olympic gymnast. *Pseudo sick day.*

She'd head upstairs, avoid her boss, grab her keys and purse, and take a trip to Carlisle to find Mason Thompson.

She hadn't worked this hard to walk away.

No, sir. Fired or not, she had a murder to solve.

JENNA PULLED INTO the driveway of Brent's home, well, the Thompson home, because now that his father had shown up, who knew what to call it?

Above her, dark clouds swirled, their blackness threatening and ugly. A storm rolling in. How appropriate. She parked and then marched next door, fighting to keep her heels from sinking into the soft grass that separated the two homes. Hopefully, Sylvie or Brent's uncle could fill her in on what had gone on with Mason. She needed to find the man, question him and compare his story to what she'd heard from the rest of Brent's family. All before Brent tracked her down.

If she thought he was mad now, all she needed to do was wait until he found her still working the case. And doing it alone. But after sneaking out of the office to avoid her boss, who would most certainly remind her that she'd been fired, Jenna and her .38 were flying solo. Besides, his family lived next door and they'd play chaperone.

Although her reasonable self warned her not to pursue this, part of her couldn't walk away. They'd come too far and it had become too personal. Proving herself wasn't the issue anymore. Now she wanted to help Brent figure out who had taken his mother from him.

She simply needed to do this one last thing and talk to Brent's father.

Then she'd either rule him out or have the sheriff question him again. And again. And again. With what Jamie had shared, it was time to pressure Mason Thompson.

Eventually, if guilty, he'd break. The man was too weak to withstand an interrogation—an *interview*—as her father called it.

Then she'd leave Brent and this case behind. For her own sake, she had to. But, darn it, the thought of that squeezed her chest, like a fist curling at the base of her throat. She heaved out a breath and pinched her eyes closed. *Don't cry.* She couldn't. Not now.

Heartbreak. That's what this was. It had been a long time since she'd felt it and—*darn*—had she ever truly understood its paralyzing presence, its savage way of sucking away every ounce of happiness? She didn't think so. Her aching body didn't either.

But she and Brent couldn't live like this. He used every disagreement as an excuse to run from a relationship, and the chaos and pain would be too much.

Just finish this. The rest she could do later. For now, she'd pull herself together and get through this last task. She tugged on the sleeves of her trench coat, smoothed the collar, took a breath and banged on Sylvie's door.

Behind her, the wind whipped up again, rattling the branches on the big oak beside the porch.

No answer.

The absence of their cars didn't bode well, but Jamie's car was here. Maybe she'd gone somewhere with Sylvie?

She banged again and waited. Still no answer. Fine. She'd try next door. Maybe Mason had returned and they were all in there having a powwow. If they weren't and Mason was there and she wound up alone with a suspected killer, well, she had her .38. That was all the reasoning she needed. She tromped down the stairs and across the lawn, her heels once again sinking into the grass. Mud on her favorite shoes. Great. Just another annoying thing on an already annoying day.

Brent had actually *fired* her. After everything they'd talked about and knowing how important this was to her, how she hungered to make a difference, he'd ripped it right out of her desperate, clutching hands.

If she could go back, maybe she'd make a different decision, ask her boss to hang on a second and call him immediately rather than waiting.

But beating it to death wouldn't fix it.

She climbed the porch and a noise—scraping—drew her attention. She peeked around the side of the house and saw the lattice Brent had torn off the other night sitting on the ground.

Hadn't he replaced that? Yes. Definitely. He'd told her that he'd only tucked it back in and would nail it in place the following weekend.

So why was it sitting on the ground? She supposed this howling wind could have knocked it off.

Unease creeped up her spine, tapping each vertebra on the way up. With each tap her heart rate kicked up. A warning? Paranoia? She continued to stare at the opening under the porch, waiting. Anticipating.

Don't.

Yet, like a lure she couldn't resist, she tiptoed off the porch to investigate. Slowly, she eased her .38 from her purse, held it just the way her father had taught her—two hands, thumbs along the side, grip tight.

She moved silently, avoiding a pile of leaves that might crunch when stepped on. No movement from under the porch. Step over step she approached. Just before the opening where the lattice should have been, she squatted.

Something flew at her—*jump*—and her pulse hammered, sending blood rocketing into her brain, slamming its way in. She reeled back. Trigger. *No.* Could be nothing. Someone clearing debris from under the house. She couldn't know. *Pull the trigger.*

Too late. A brick—another damned brick—hit her square in the chest, knocking the wind out of her. She fell backward, landing on her butt, and pain shot down both legs. Gasping, she forced air into her lungs. Gun. *Don't drop it.*

Before she could look up, another brick smashed down onto her hand. Grinding hot pain lanced into her fingers and she cried out. Looming over her was Jamie—*Jamie?*—brick still in hand, readying for another swing. *Fight.* Jenna kicked out, connected with Jamie's hip, knocking Jamie sideways.

Somehow, her gun was still in her hand, but her grip was no good. She tried to curl her fingers and a second bolt of pain shot through them. Useless fingers. She rolled, grabbed the gun with her left hand and—*boom!*—something clocked her on the back of the head.

Ahead of her a tree swayed, its edges blurring against the gray sky. Using a branch as a focal point, she got to her knees. Nausea filled her belly. *Feel sick.* Cold, wet moisture from the dirt seeped through her tights to her knees, and her head looped and spun right along with her rebelling stomach. *Too much.*

She lay back down and closed her eyes. *No sleeping.* She fought to open her eyes but the lids were so heavy.

"Stupid beauty queen," Jamie said. "My cousin loses his sense and look where we are. So stupid." Something poked Jenna's side. "Get up."

Up? No. She closed her eyes again. Sighed at the relief. And then, finally, the blackness came.

"HE'S BACK?" CAMILLE asked, her voice cracking under the strain of hearing that their father had appeared as suddenly as he'd abandoned them nine years earlier.

Brent sat back on his sister's giant sofa and forced his shoulders into a relaxed position. In the time he'd been working his mother's case, this was one conversation he never wanted to have, but if he appeared calm, Camille might believe it.

Typically, he could talk motives and suspects with no problem. Telling Camille their father had returned would open the gaping wound she'd spent years of therapy gluing shut.

Brent nodded. "He showed up at the house today. Uncle Herb talked to him. Sylvie is a mess and I'm heading out there. I wanted you to know."

At least *she* wouldn't be blindsided.

Get over it. He couldn't dwell on the fact that he and Jenna, despite their raging sexual attraction, didn't mesh. If they had, she would have notified him lickety-split about his father. Even if she didn't know the old man was moving up the time frame, she should have told Brent he was coming. Sure, the guy showing up a day early would have been a surprise, but Brent would have at least known he was coming.

Instead, he got smacked upside the head with it and still didn't understand why.

Women. Always complicating his life.

His phone rang. *Ignore it.* He drummed his fingers on his leg and Camille's gaze shot to the coffee table where his phone continued to ring.

"Is that him?"

"I don't know. Could be. Uncle Herb gave him my number."

"Can I look?"

Third ring. "Sure."

Shaking her head, Camille scooped the phone up and glanced at the screen. "Penny Hennings."

Brent blew air through his lips and gave the relief its due diligence. Facing his father was imminent, but he didn't have to rush it. Had it been Mason calling, Brent would have ignored it. Let the old man wait on him for a change.

The phone went silent and Camille set it down. "Isn't she Jenna's boss?"

"She is."

"Maybe they have news. Shouldn't you talk to her?"

"I fired them."

As expected, because his sister's mannerisms hadn't changed since her seventh birthday, she wrinkled her nose and pursed her lips. Total pig face. "Why?"

Where should he start? "Jenna sat on telling me about Dad. He wasn't due until tomorrow."

Camille shrugged. "And?"

And nothing. "She should've called me ASAP."

"But…" She cocked her head. "You just said he wasn't due until tomorrow. You're mad because she didn't call you?"

When she put it that way, it didn't sound reasonable. "It's not that simple."

"Brent, you're my big brother and I've always been in awe of you, but that's dumb."

"Hey—"

"No hey. If it had been me having to deliver that message, I'd have needed a few minutes to figure out how to tell you our deadbeat father was back. I'd have been worried about your reaction, and I know you better than anyone. She cares about you and you fired her." Brent leaned forward, but Camille held her hands up. "I'm not saying she was right, but she's done a lot for us. That's all."

Camille was taking Jenna's side. What the hell was with his family?

"I *don't* like being blindsided."

"But she didn't blindside you. Dad did. It's his fault, not hers."

His voice mail chirped and that reprieve couldn't have come at a better time considering that Camille and her ever-efficient mind were aggravating him. He picked up his phone, checked the screen because why not? This conversation was definitely skidding off the rails.

"You want to run from her," Camille said.

He'd scroll through his emails while he was at it.

"Brent, you know I love you, but there's a reason you're not attached, and running won't cure it."

Enough. He met his sister's gaze, gave her the hard look he knew she'd understand. "Shut up about my life."

His normally agreeable sister shrugged. "You've never shut up about my life."

Hello? Someone had to take care of her. He hit the button to dial Penny.

Camille rolled her eyes. "You're messing this up. And that would be a shame because I think you care about her. I never butt into your business when it comes to women, but this time it won't be so easy for you to walk away."

Brent held the phone up. "It's ringing."

And I'm ignoring you. At least trying to. When had his sister gotten so smart about people? About *him*? He'd give her credit for one thing, she had him nailed. Yes, he'd walk away from Jenna, and no, it wouldn't be easy.

Nothing was ever easy when it came to Jenna. Especially that crazy feeling he got every time she stepped into his orbit. When she was close, he wanted closer. There was comfort there. A connection he'd never had and...*forget it.* No sense in tormenting himself.

Penny picked up. "Hey," he said into the phone. "What's up?"

"Is Jenna with you?"

His fingertips tingled. Weird. He curled and uncurled his free hand. Brent stood and paced the small area behind the sofa. "Uh, no. I left her in the lobby. Why?"

"Because she's gone."

"Gone where?"

"Well, Brent, if I knew, I wouldn't be asking you. She's not answering her cell. You said she's in danger and now she's gone."

He stopped pacing, stared straight ahead while his pulse jackhammered. *She's gone. AWOL.* He wouldn't panic. Not yet. Jenna liked going rogue and he wouldn't put it past her to continue investigating. Even after he'd canned her. Her relentless ambition, her quest to find answers, were things he loved about her. Chances were she'd bolted to avoid Penny asking questions.

"I'll find her."

He hung up on Penny and dialed Jenna's number.

"Problem?" Camille asked.

"Jenna went AWOL."

"After you fired her."

He adored his sister, but right now she was hacking at his last stable nerve. "You need to back off."

She hopped off the chair, walked to the entryway of the tiny apartment and grabbed her coat off the hook.

Jenna's voice mail beeped and her voice, the breathy one she layered on when she thought she needed it, came through the line.

"It's me," he said. "Call me."

Camille shrugged into her coat. "No answer?"

"No. Where are you going?"

"Wherever you are. It's time to find our father."

Chapter Fourteen

"Wake up, beauty queen."

Still with her eyes closed and fighting the need to come fully awake, Jenna focused on the voice. *Who is that?* Piercing light flashed behind her eyelids and a shattering stab blazed down her neck. She peeled open her eyes, met the darkened living room of the Thompson's house and silently thanked whatever god had gifted her with dim lighting.

Ratty sneakers appeared in front of her. Jenna slid her gaze upward, along the jean-clad legs, over the zip-up jacket—Jamie—to the .38 in the woman's hand.

My gun.

Jenna, the FBI reject, had made the most critical of all critical errors and let her weapon leave her. *So sorry, Dad.* Worse, she didn't understand any of this. She rolled to her back and her vision loopy-looped right along with her stomach. *Gonna be sick.* "Bathroom."

Jamie squatted in front of her. "What?"

"I'm…sick."

"Yeah. Expected that when I dragged you in here." She dropped a small pail next to Jenna. "Here you go, beauty queen. Do your thing."

Swallowing back bile, she clutched at the pail, waiting. She exhaled, then inhaled again and still vomit threatened.

After a few more breaths, she opened her eyes and slid her gaze sideways. Jamie stood by the window.

"What are you doing?" Jenna asked.

"You don't want to know."

Get up. If she could just sit up, maybe she'd have a chance to get the gun back. *Fool.* She could barely see straight, much less fight for a gun big enough to knock a decent-sized hole in her. Still, if the alternative was lying on this floor waiting for someone to save her, she'd better figure out a plan.

Jenna levered up and found herself on the losing end of her own gun. Vomit lurched into her throat and—*oh, no, oh, no*—she grabbed the pail, heaving into it, gagging until her eyeballs wanted to burst.

Maybe she'd need that hero after all.

She lolled back against the sofa and her stomach contracted, released and contracted again. Now that her stomach had emptied, maybe the nausea would subside. Let her at least get to her feet.

She stared down at the plastic bucket Jamie must have retrieved from next door. The pungent odor of pine needles invaded her already vulnerable system and she sat back, held her arm against her nose to block the smell.

Her fingers throbbed from the bashing they'd taken with the brick and she flexed them, wincing along the way. None broken. One good thing. "Jamie, please. Tell me what's happening."

"That idiot uncle of mine came back. That's what's happening. He's been gone all this time. You come along and suddenly he's back. You love that, don't you? Men falling at your feet. Following your every command." She let out a frustrated grunt. "Stupid beauty queen."

Jenna studied her movements. Stiff, jerky, nervous.

And holding a gun.

She met her gaze and those eyes that were almost the

exact color of Brent's and Sylvie's and all she saw was death. "I don't know what you're doing, but please, put that gun down before someone gets hurt."

"Shut up."

Setting the pail next to her, Jenna hung on to the edge in case she needed to swing it. "Can I get off the floor?"

Jamie held up the gun, gestured to the sofa. "Fine. On the couch. Move slow. It won't be much longer."

"For what?"

"For our visitor. My uncle is coming. He will confess to murdering my aunt and after I catch him with your dead body, I'll shoot him in self-defense. Then it's all over. Everyone goes back to their lives."

Prickles of panic cruised along Jenna's skin.

Unglued.

This whole setup was to get her uncle here so she could stage a murder. Jamie's hand shook and her gaze bounced around.

Jenna eyed the door, calculated the time it would take to get there.

"I need this to end," Jamie said. "This house should be razed so we can get on with our lives and stop thinking about Cheryl. It's all anybody cares about. This empty house and Cheryl. Now I'm going to end it. Once and for all."

Jenna's panic took hold and she pictured the scene. Bodies in front of the sofa, blood everywhere. Brent would find them. He'd walk in, see the bodies and it would be a miracle if he didn't go insane. A fierce protective instinct whipped at her.

"This isn't the way. If your uncle murdered your aunt, let the sheriff deal with him. *This* will not help you."

"Yeah, it will. You have no idea."

And the look in her eyes, that cold, deadly calm left Jenna wondering if a killer stood in front of her.

Next plan. Jenna pushed off the floor, her stomach flopping like a fish on land. And dummy her, she'd come out here and not told anyone. So many mistakes.

At the entryway, her purse had been thrown against the wall. Jamie must have put it there when she'd dragged her inside. Some of the contents, the tools of her trade—hairbrush, lipstick, notepad—had fallen out and lay scattered on the floor.

"Forget it," Jamie said. "I took your phone. My cousin keeps calling. He hates when people don't return his calls."

She didn't know that, but could use it. "I do know. I should call him. He's such a worrier. I told him I was coming here. If I don't call him, he'll break speed records."

Jamie waved the gun. "I listened to your voice mail. He's mad at you, beauty queen. Demanding to know where you are."

Caught. "He'll figure it out."

"Maybe." She shrugged. "By the time he gets here, all he'll find is another dead woman. And his dead father." She spun to the window and stormed around, jabbing the .38 once, twice, three times in Jenna's direction. Each time, Jenna flinched, waiting for the bang of an accidental—or not so accidental—shot.

"Jamie, please. I don't understand. If Mason is guilty, you committing a double murder doesn't accomplish anything. All it does is get you a life sentence."

Even if her plan was to make Mason look guilty.

"And dispose of a killer."

"But at what cost?"

"Doesn't matter."

Totally snapped. Not a pinch of rational thought to be found. Jenna rested her pounding head against the back of the sofa and faced off with her own gun. Her thoughts whirled and she analyzed her errors, picking them apart with brutal accuracy. Coming here alone, not alerting anyone, her failure to move when the brick flew at her.

But wait. Jamie hadn't been here when they'd found the bricks. Jenna ticked back to their conversation at the truck stop. She hadn't said anything. She had, in fact, put her off.

"You tossed the brick through my window, didn't you?"

No answer.

"Why, Jamie?"

Again no answer. *Push her.*

"To scare me off, right? Only I didn't go. Then I found your uncle."

"And brought him back here. As if we needed that filth here after he left his children? What kind of man abandons his children after their mother is murdered? *Not* my father. That's for sure."

The way she said it, accentuating the *not*, caught Jenna sideways. *Odd.* "What does that mean?"

"*My* father is a good man. He takes care of us. Whatever his faults, he never walked away. So I'm going to fix things. Finally make them right."

Jenna's vision blurred again and she swallowed another surge of bile. Her stomach protested and she grabbed the bucket, heaving into it. Sick as a dog, head spinning and Jamie off her rocker. With Jenna's gun. Outside, a clap of thunder sounded and the boom rattled the windows.

Banner afternoon.

Jenna finished with the bucket and, short on options, dabbed the cuff of her sweater against her mouth. "I could use a napkin. I have some in my purse. Please?"

"Is this a trick?"

It wasn't, but the idea had merit. If she could distract Jamie, she might get a few seconds to attack. But with the way her head spun, she'd probably fall on her face. "Please. I'm so sick."

Jamie rolled her eyes. "Now you're a drama queen on top

of a beauty queen. I expected more from you." She stomped to Jenna's purse and kicked it toward her. "You get them. And don't try anything. I *will* shoot you."

Jenna didn't doubt that.

A car door slammed, the sound muffled by the closed door. "Finally," Jamie huffed. Keeping the weapon aimed at Jenna, she peeked out the window.

"You're about to meet Brent's father."

Jamie cracked the door ajar, waiting for Mason to push it open. *This is it.* Heavy footsteps—boots—thunked against the wood and Jamie inched back, raising the gun. *Do something, do something, do something.*

"Run!" Jenna screamed. "Run!"

Jamie swung right, the .38 looming in Jenna's direction and—*don't shoot, please don't shoot*—Jamie's finger moved over the trigger. *Go.* Jenna rolled sideways. *Boom!* The shot ripped into the arm of the sofa where Jenna had just been sitting. *Stone-cold crazy.*

Jamie swung the gun back to the doorway. Standing there, a look of terror and panic tightening his cheeks, stood Brent's father. It may as well have been Brent in thirty years. Same big build, same hair color and bone structure.

Bone structure she definitely wanted to see in thirty years.

No dying today.

Jenna scrambled to her feet, the soles of her shoes slipping on the damned wood and her bad ankle barked. No traction. "Run!"

"Don't move," Jamie said, calm as could be. She backed up. "I don't care which one of you I kill first. Anyone moves, they get shot." She jerked her head at Mason. "Get inside."

The idiot stood in the doorway, hands raised. This man was Brent's father? Something went fluky in the gene pool. Brent would have disarmed her in four seconds. Maybe three. His father? He froze. She supposed Jamie was right about one thing: Mason Thompson was a weak man.

"Inside or I shoot you. I don't care. You're worthless anyway."

Run. Please, run. Get help. This time she hoped he'd run for the right reasons.

He stepped inside and Jenna gasped.

"Shut that door and lock it," Jamie said.

Again, Mason did as he was told.

"What the hell's going on, Jamie?" he asked.

Jamie tilted her head. "Oh, Uncle Mason, we're going to play a little game. It's called Let's-Make-Everything-Right. Now get in here and shut up."

BRENT SWUNG INTO the driveway, spotted Jenna's car parked in front of a blue pickup with a missing tailgate and let out a stream of curses that would put Aunt Sylvie in a straitjacket.

His father always drove pickups and although Brent had never seen this one, he didn't doubt who it belonged to.

So, yeah, Jenna was inside the house, probably interviewing his father. After Brent had fired her.

"I see Jenna took that whole you're-fired thing seriously," Camille cracked.

Another smart-mouth. Lucky him. He jammed the SUV into Park and eyeballed his sister. "You about done?"

"Not nearly. I always let you take the lead on things, but this time, I think you're in over your head. It doesn't matter at this minute, though, because I'd like to see what our father is up to."

"You want me to do this? I could talk to him and then bring you in."

Camille's dark blue eyes clouded and grew darker. Intense. *Stronger.* Normally, he'd insist on handling this himself. But hadn't that been one of Jenna's observations? That he never let anyone help him?

"No," Camille said. "I'm tired of being afraid to face him."

Brent reached over and tugged on her hair the way he used to when she was a kid. Those were the good memories, the memories that reminded him that their childhood hadn't been a complete loss. "Let's do it, then."

He slid from the SUV, contemplated throwing his suit jacket on again. Nah. Why make an effort for a guy who'd walked out on them?

In the distance, thunder rumbled. Wicked storm heading in. They'd make this quick and get back on the road again.

He stopped in front of the car, grabbed Camille's arm and looked her in the eyes, searching, making sure this is what she wanted.

His sister patted his hand. "I'm okay. I've got you and you've got me. That's all we need. We take care of each other."

Yes, they did. Whatever their childhood had tossed at them, they'd survived. "That we do, sis."

Camille pointed to the driveway next door. "Jamie is here. I wonder if they're all inside with him."

Him. Brent didn't expect a lot from his life, but he never wanted to reach a place where his children would refer to their father as *him* rather than Dad. A sad state all around.

Brent dragged a hand over his face. "I can't handle all of them. Not in this lifetime. It'll be a free-for-all. We have to clear the place so you and I can talk to him. Back me up on that."

"You know I will."

Camille tucked her arm into his and the two of them walked toward the porch. "Don't be mad at Jenna. She's invested. You can't hold that against her."

Brent snorted. "Is this some twisted female unity?"

"Maybe. I like her. She'd be good for you. If you pulled your head out of your rear."

"Don't start."

He unhooked his arm, dragged his key from his pocket and tromped up the stairs. He wouldn't knock. Never. He'd maintained this house for years. His name wasn't on the deed, but he'd assumed responsibility. Whatever was going on in that house, it involved him. And Camille.

He shoved the key in the door, flipped the lock and grabbed the knob. For a brief second the cold metal against his sweat-soaked palm shocked him. When he opened the door, he'd put eyes on his father for the first time in over nine years. No visits or calls or wondering if they were all right.

Nine years.

A fresh bout of anger hissed at him, coiled around his neck and he stiffened. *Stay calm.* That's what he needed now. Not to blow his top. To treat his father with respectful indifference. That's all the old man would get. Brent cracked his neck, rolled his shoulders and all that coiling anger loosened its grip. *Better.* He turned the knob and gently pushed open the door.

"Gun!"

Jenna's voice. One second. That's how long it took the word to register. Gun. Someone inside had a gun. And it wasn't Jenna. *Cover.* He shoved Camille sideways, drew his weapon and spun away from the door. Breathing deep, he zeroed in on a tree branch smacking around. Inside, Jenna's yelling mixed with another female voice, the words muddling together. *Don't shoot. Back up. It's Brent.* What in hell was going on?

Drowning in a blood rush, he glanced at the gun in his trembling hands. Dammit. Between practice and even discharging it while on duty, he'd held this gun countless times. Never once had his hands shook.

"Shut up!"

Jamie.

"Brent," Jenna yelled, "Jamie has my gun."

A shot, loud and booming went off. *No, no, no.* Who the hell was Jamie shooting at? The front window shattered and glass flew, sprinkling down on Camille, who was still stretched on the worn porch floor. *Please, don't let her be hit.*

Camille covered her head with her hands. *She's moving.* "Are you hit?"

His sister looked up at him, her normally big eyes even wider and...spooked. Shock. "Camille," he snapped, "are you okay?"

"Yes."

Another burst of adrenaline, relief this time, flooded his system. "Get off this porch. Run."

"I'm not leaving you."

"Brent?" Jamie's voice came from inside.

He rested his head against the house, his blood still barreling, scrambling his thoughts. What the hell was going on? *Disarm her. No. Hold perimeter.*

How?

He couldn't deal with it alone. He'd need backup. *Wait for the sheriff.* No chances. Not with Jenna and apparently his father inside.

Being held at gunpoint.

By his cousin.

Couldn't be.

"Jamie, please. Tell me what's happening."

"I'm sorry, Brent. I'm so sorry. I didn't mean for it to go this way."

Three seconds ago, he'd doubted his cousin could be holding that gun. Three seconds ago, he wouldn't have believed that his sweet, caring cousin, who'd helped him through countless jams in his lifetime, could fire a weapon. Three seconds ago, he'd thought he knew all there was to know about Jamie.

In three short seconds, his illusions had disintegrated and this thing launched to another level.

He dialed into his law enforcement training and blocked out his emotions. There was no room for them. Now, he was a stranger, a US marshal doing his job and addressing this situation.

To his right, Camille had moved to all fours. "Get off the porch. I need backup. Go call 9-1-1. Do it. Now."

Her gaze ping-ponged between him and the door. "Go," he said.

Finally, she crawled to the porch steps, staying clear of the open doorway. "I'll get help and come back."

Not in his lifetime. "No. Stay clear. See if Aunt Sylvie and Uncle Herb are home."

All he needed was his aunt and uncle barging in on the middle of this thing, wanting answers. Hell, he wanted answers. "If they're home, make sure they don't come here. Now go. Stay low in front of the house."

Brent watched her, his heart banging, slamming against him as his baby sister, who he'd protected from childhood, duck-walked across the lawn and out of a bullet's path. *Stay low, please stay low.* She cleared the lawn and Brent let out a small breath. *Little farther.* Driveway clear. *Check.* She made it to his aunt's house and he rested his head back. The blood rush turned to a trickle and he cut his gaze left and right.

"Jamie?" he yelled.

"Come inside, Brent."

Instinct pushed him forward. Nothing odd there, given his protective tendencies. Jamie knew this about him. She *expected* it. Law enforcement training and all those hard-fought lessons about never entering a situation like this alone kept him still.

The sheriff would show up in minutes. Before that, Brent needed to keep everyone calm. And get Jenna's .38 out of

Jamie's extremely unskilled hands. He breathed in and focused on the banging tree branch. *Go time.*

"James, put that gun down." Using his cousin's childhood nickname couldn't hurt. "I'm not coming inside until you put the gun down. Or you come out here and let me see you."

"No."

Another wind gust blew the tree branches sideways, smacking them against the house—*crack*—and making him flinch. Then came another round of thunder, closer this time and booming. Brent glanced at the sky where thick black clouds rolled in. Anytime now the sky would open up and soak the place. If it kept Camille and his aunt and uncle next door, he'd deal with it.

"Brent?" Jamie hollered.

"Let Jenna and my dad come out. They come out and I come in."

"No."

"James, come on."

"No."

"Who's in there with you?"

"Just the beauty queen and your useless father."

How the hell had things gotten so out of control that it had come to this? The woman he loved was trapped inside. Trapped with his father, a man Brent hadn't yet reconciled his feelings about and now they could both die.

Brent leaned his head against the house. *Diversion.* If he could distract Jamie, he'd get a chance to disarm her and figure out what happened.

"Okay," he hollered. "We don't want your folks in the middle of this, right?"

"Brent! You keep them out of here."

"I will, James. I will. Give me five minutes, okay?"

"Five minutes!"

"Promise me you won't do anything stupid."

Anything else stupid.

"I won't. As long as the beauty queen and your father stay put. Do not call the sheriff, Brent. I'll kill them both if you do."

Kill them. What? Jamie? He squeezed his eyes shut, felt the pressure in his forehead. Work the problem and fix this. He gripped the gun again—too tight—then loosened his hold. "Nobody will come in there that you don't want. I promise."

Brent tore off down the porch steps, keeping low as he crossed the lawn. Camille came from the front of Aunt Sylvie's, met him by the driveway, and he steered her around the side of the house. "They home?"

"No. I called the sheriff. He's over by Johnson's farm dealing with a wreck. He and a deputy are on the way, but it'll be fifteen minutes before they get here. Where are we going?"

"Basement."

"Why?"

"We're creating a diversion."

Chapter Fifteen

On the list of things to be thankful for, an outside basement entrance just flew to the top. Brent holstered his gun and hustled down the concrete steps where, using slow, silent movements, he turned the knob on the door.

"What—" Camille whispered.

"Shh."

She closed her mouth and Brent held his fingers against his lips. Above them, thunder boomed again. Using the noise as cover, he pushed open the door. The musty smell hit him full force.

On one side, his father's old tools still littered the top of the workbench. Next to the bench was the rolling tool chest. He'd need that. The furnace, with its newly installed gas line, was in the right corner. Beside it was his target. The hot-water heater.

He spun back to Camille. "Get me the wire cutters from the tool chest. And a hammer. If there's no hammer, give me something I can bang on this safety valve with. Do it quietly."

The floors were thin and any odd noise would echo right into the upper floor. He glanced around looking for a rag, a garden bag, anything that would muffle the sound when he jammed the safety valve. Nothing. He started unbuttoning his shirt, stripping down to his undershirt.

Camille gave him a look. "Uh, what are you doing?"

"I'm about to crush the safety valve so it won't work and I need to muffle the bang."

"What?"

"Shh."

He balled his shirt, set it on top of the valve and felt through the fabric to make sure his aim was square. She handed him a hammer. *Whack.* He blasted it. One good muffled shot. Excellent. He set the hammer down and shut the cold-water valve.

"Brent?"

"Give me a sec. I helped Dad replace a hot-water heater once. He told me all the things I shouldn't do. I'm doing them."

He squatted, gave the water-release valve a spin and water sloshed out, pouring over his shoes and the floor. Soaked. Dammit.

Camille still held the wire cutters and he waggled his fingers. Better than any surgical nurse, she slapped them into his hand. He grasped the red wire linking the temperature control knob to the sensor. *Snip.* That's gone. Quickly, he whipped the temp-control knob to its highest setting and the burner flamed all the way open.

He checked the water still pouring out of the tank. *Not enough.* But he had to get back upstairs. Camille.

He jumped up and faced his sister. "I need your help."

"Anything."

"Wait another five minutes, then shut the water valve. We need this thing half full. It usually takes ten minutes. If you wait another four or five, it should be good enough. Then you need to get the hell out of here because the top of this water heater will blow straight off. Hopefully, it'll scare the hell out of Jamie and I can disarm her."

"Are you insane?"

He had to be because he was leaving his baby sister

down here to practically set off his homemade bomb. God help him if something happened to her. He'd never live with it.

He stepped back. "Forget it. You can't do this. Too dangerous. I'll think of something else."

"What?"

"I don't know."

Camille glanced at the hot water heater.

"Forget it, Camille."

But she waggled her head. "It's the only option. Besides, you've done most of the work. If we do it this way, in a few minutes, this will all be over. I can do it."

"Camille—"

She spun on him and pointed. "Stop. I can do this. It's the only way everyone gets out safely. Just tell me what to do."

Dug in. When his sister got like this, it took a bulldozer to move her. And short on options, they'd have to go with it.

"Get your phone out," he said. "Watch the time. No longer than five minutes. I don't want you in here when this thing blows. I'd do it myself, but I gotta get back up there."

She shooed him away. "Leave. I'll find you."

"When you leave here, go next door. If Sylvie and Herb come home, make sure they stay there. That's what I need from you. Got it?"

His sister hesitated. *Nuh-uh.* "Camille?"

Finally she nodded. "I've got it. We can do this."

KEEPING HER GAZE pinned to Jamie—and the .38—Jenna leaned her head against the arm of the sofa. *I need to do something.* Clearly Brent's father was content to do nothing. Total gene-pool malfunction. And thank God for that because if she knew Brent even a little bit, he had a plan.

Only problem with that was Jamie knew Brent better than Jenna and had probably come to the same conclusion.

"James?" Brent shouted from the porch.

Jamie swung her head to the still-open door and immediately came back to Jenna.

"Hey," Jenna said. "Stop swinging that gun around before it accidentally goes off and hits one of us. Then your problems get a whole lot worse."

"Shut up!"

"Jamie," Brent hollered, "I'm coming in."

Jenna sat up, half relieved, half terrified. Growing up with a houseful of cops she knew an officer should never—ever—enter a situation like this without backup. Which meant either Brent had backup or he'd chosen to wing it.

Then he was in the doorway, feet spread, arms up, gun aimed at Jamie. This family. Tragic from the get-go.

The back of Jenna's neck itched and her arms tingled. Add that to the pounding headache and her body went more than a little berserk. Jamie stood faced off with Brent. If he could keep her occupied, Jenna might be able to lunge and draw her attention. Between the two of them, they'd get that gun. Hopefully before someone wound up with a hole in them.

Jamie looked back. "Don't move."

Jenna held her hands up. "Sorry. Sorry."

"Sit still, Jenna," Brent said.

Mason was beside her, his long legs stretched in front of him, arms at his sides. Brent glanced in his direction but quickly averted his eyes. "Anyone hurt?"

"We're okay," Jenna said.

There were hundreds—thousands—of ways this situation could end. Another shot being fired was only one of them. *Get the gun.*

Brent took a step into the room.

"Stay there," Jamie said.

"Talk to me. Whatever this is, we can fix. No one is hurt. James, please, we can fix this."

"I didn't want it."

"I know," he said. "Whatever happened, we'll fix it. Put the gun down."

"Brent!" a woman shouted from outside, her voice edged with crackling panic.

Camille.

Footsteps pounded against the porch—*thunk, thunk, thunk*—and in stormed Brent's aunt and uncle.

Included in those thousand ways the situation could go bad would be Brent's aunt and uncle rushing in.

"Get out!" Jamie shrieked, the high-pitched wail tearing through the tense air like a buzz saw against cardboard.

Gun still on Jamie, Brent jerked his head. "All of you, out."

Herb stepped forward. These people. Insanity.

"What in the hell are you doing?" he asked his daughter.

"Leave, Dad."

"I will not. Put that thing down."

Boom! Something under them—not close, by the kitchen—exploded and Jenna glanced through the archway following the sound. A loud scream mixed with the explosion. Jenna's ears whistled. Thirty feet away, an object blasted through the kitchen floor, sending the old linoleum flying, hunks of it showering down.

Jamie stood in front of her, mouth agape, her body angled toward the mess. *Get the gun.* Scrambling to her feet, Jenna lunged. Brent was faster. Her gaze cut to him and she leaped out of the way as his big body crashed down on top of Jamie. The gun hit the floor with a *thwack.* Brent swatted it, sending it in Jenna's direction.

She scooped it up. "Got it."

Under Brent, Jamie bucked and kicked and hollered.

I'm done.

Jenna trained the weapon on Jamie. "Stop. Right now."

"Shoot me. Do it. Please."

Oh, she'd like the chance. Yes, she would. And in that

moment, in her state of mind, she'd do it. She'd let go of any inhibition because this woman had planned on killing her. And leaving her body for Brent to find. How she— someone who supposedly loved this man—could allow him to walk into this house and find more bodies, Jenna couldn't grasp. The terror it would have inflicted upon his already shattered world would have driven him mad. And that, Jenna wouldn't stand for.

"If you don't stop moving I will. And don't think I won't. You were going to let him walk in here and find us. That makes you a monster. I hate monsters."

"Everyone, shut up," Brent said, his huge body still locking Jamie down. "Jamie, I will lay here all night if I have to." He grabbed both her wrists and pinned them. "Stop."

Under his substantial weight, she finally gave in, succumbed to the idea that she couldn't fight him off. "Dad, help me."

"Help you?" her father screamed, his eyes fixed and horrified. "I don't know what you're doing. How am I supposed to help you?"

"Uncle Herb," Brent said, "take Aunt Sylvie outside. Check on Camille and stay with them. Please."

Turning on his heel, Herb grabbed Sylvie by the elbow, ushering her out. Jamie's eyes bulged as her cheeks hardened.

"You're turning your back on me?" she shrieked as her parents left the house. "After what you did to those women?"

What women? Something prickled at the base of Jenna's neck.

"Dad, please."

And then the tears came. Jamie dropped her head, laying her cheek against the wooden floor, shrieking as if a limb had been severed. "I did it for him. Whatever he did to those women, I did it for him."

Jenna moved closer, keeping the gun on Jamie, but glancing at Brent. He met her gaze, but his eyes, the look there, all that nothingness—just lifeless—slammed her, made her ache for him. She set her hand on his shoulder and squeezed. "Baby, you need to get up. I've got this."

Brent eased off his cousin, but kept one knee on her back.

"It's okay," Jenna said. "I have her. Take a breath. I have her."

IN HIS LIFE, there had been moments of bewilderment, moments of disappointment, moments of life-shattering agony that cut so deep he knew he'd never recover.

This would be all of those moments combined.

Lifting his knee from Jamie, Brent backed away, his mind spinning, working, considering. All of it coming at him in a rush, making him dizzy and…confused.

"Brent?"

Jenna. She stood, gun in hand, making sure the situation stayed calm. She drove him crazy, but how many women could go through what she'd just experienced and still manage to stay in control.

"I'm okay," he said.

A lie, but he'd lied about his emotional state before. His cousin continued to wail on the floor and his mind reeled back twenty-three years. The back door. No one but family ever used the back door. *I did it for him.* Jamie's words lingered, but like a language he didn't understand, a disconnect existed.

"Jamie, why are you crying? What did you do?"

"The clothes," she shrieked, tears streaming down her face. "The clothes in the basement. I saw them. Your mom saw when he burned them."

A frigid grip took hold and Brent shivered. He stepped back, steadying himself. *Let her talk.*

"I heard her ask about them. She wouldn't let it go."

"Oh, God," Camille said.

Camille. Brent spun, saw his sister in the doorway. Whatever this was, she didn't need to hear it. "Out!"

"What did you do?" Camille repeated.

"I wanted to protect him. That's all. I didn't mean…"

"Everyone stop talking," Jenna said. "Right now."

She's right. Brent didn't care. He could do this. With Aunt Sylvie and Uncle Herb outside, he could control the emotional chaos in the house and get answers. He squatted next to Jamie, reminded himself that she'd been a constant supporter since his mom died and set his hand on her back. "Sit up and talk to me. Tell me what happened. What clothes in the basement?"

Facing away from him, Jamie rested her cheek against the floor, her hair fanning out. "The women's clothes. When he comes home, he hides them behind the pipe in the basement. Then he burns them. He gets rid of them. I didn't know why and then I figured it out. He killed the women and burned their clothes. It's always when he comes home from a trip. I used to watch for him. He'd come home and go to the basement first. I went down there one morning and found the clothes. When I got home from school, they were gone and he was cleaning the fire pit. He'd burn them in the fire pit when we weren't around."

"Brent," Jenna said, "please stop this. She should have a lawyer. You need to do this the right way."

"Yes. Stop this." The sheriff strode through the door, gun drawn, a deputy on his heels. "All of you, outside."

"I didn't mean to kill her," Jamie said, still on the floor. "But she caught him. She caught him burning the clothes and I got scared."

Someone latched on to the back of Brent's shirt. Jenna.

"You shouldn't be in here," she said.

He squared his shoulders, but inside the torture ran hot

and deep, ripping into him, making his mind burn with visions of his cousin, his beloved cousin, swinging that brick at his mother. All to protect his uncle.

Leave. This house was a curse. Every sickening inch of it. *Leave.* He glanced at his father, sitting on that damned floor and the fury Brent had kept under wraps for so long unraveled, whipping inside him like a live wire, its tip singeing him. As much as he didn't want his father dead, the man had left them. Left *him* to care for a teenaged girl. How the hell would they fix this?

Could they fix it?

Jenna gave him a not-so-light shove and his feet moved. One foot, then the next, heading to the door where there would be fresh air and the howling wind and hopefully a ton a rain. Enough rain to wash away this house and the horror that it kept ramming down his throat.

I'm losing it.

He got to the porch and—yes—violent, fat raindrops poured from the sky. Rain so hard that it pounded against the roof—hammering and hammering—like it would drill through the shingles. Let it. Let it soak the house. Drown it.

He jogged down the stairs, swung a left and stormed to the backyard.

"Brent?" his aunt called from somewhere behind him.

"No," Jenna hollered back, pausing to turn back. "Give him a minute."

His aunt screamed, her hysterics registering and Brent stopped.

Jenna nudged him forward. "Keep moving. I just looked and there's a deputy with them. Camille is there, too. You need a break."

Protecting him. His feet kept moving, his shoes sinking into the already soft grass. He needed out. That's all he knew. A few minutes of peace and no one depending on him to save them.

He reached the backyard and hooked another left, pacing the rear of the house praying to God his family wouldn't come back here and see him like this.

When he reached the far end of the house he turned back and his gaze connected with Jenna's. She stood by the tree outside of his old room, the rain dousing her, making her normally pristine hair cling to her head. She took one step and her heel stuck in the mud. She kicked off her shoes—*I love this woman*—and walked toward him, her feet sinking in the muddy grass.

"It was her," he said, sliding a sideways glance at Jenna as he stomped by, continuing to pace, just burning off the energy searing him from inside out. "She sat with us at every holiday knowing what she'd done. That she'd wrecked us. All this time."

At the edge of the house, he turned again, did another lap. Jenna struggled to keep up and finally stopped in the middle by the back porch.

"Let it out, Brent. Please. Just let it fly. You'll feel better."

He'd feel better? Really? He didn't think so, because all that fire and rage and pain was tearing through him. His arms, legs, stomach. Each body part shredding. He'd trusted Jamie, looked up to her for helping to care for them. For showing them how loving families stepped up and gave shelter when all else failed. He *loved* her.

And she'd murdered his mother.

A fifteen-year-old murderer. How the hell?

He turned for another lap, slid a glance at Jenna and his throat started to close. Jamie had held on to this secret, letting him obsess and give up his life to search for a killer. She'd watched him torment himself and never cared.

Breathe, breathe, breathe.

He walked faster. *Keep moving. Breathe.* The shredding continued. No escape. Nowhere to put it all.

"Brent, let it out."

He spun and faced Jenna and his mind went all kinds of crazy. "What was she talking about? My uncle killed women? *She* killed my mother?"

The words—were they even words?—turned into a howl. Like a hole had been blown open and all that rage poured out of his mouth. Agony, every second of it, and the pressure behind his eyes became too much. He dug the palms of his hands against them and continued the insane screaming. *I'm cracking up*.

"I'm going to touch you," Jenna said, somehow penetrating his yelling.

A second went by and she rested her hand on his back. It stuck to his now soaked shirt, but she rubbed back and forth. "It's okay," she said. "Let it out."

Maybe it was the softness in her voice or that magic touch of hers, but the howling stopped and the air went silent. Over. That fast, just done.

A crack of thunder boomed again, but Jenna kept rubbing. "You're okay. Come sit on the porch."

She took his hand and led him to the porch. Her feet sloshed in the wet grass, but she kept moving until she shoved him to a step. Exhaustion leveled him and he dropped his head, allowing himself a few seconds. A few more.

Breathe.

Jenna sat next to him and rested her head on his shoulder. "You'll be okay," she said.

He glanced at her, soaked to the skin, her makeup dripping down her cheeks into the wet bandage on her face— she'd need a dry one—and he knew she was right. For the first time in twenty-three years, looking down at this beautiful woman who'd probably drive him to madness, he knew he'd be okay.

Chapter Sixteen

By 7:00 p.m. Jenna was still at her desk supposedly working on an expense report that should have taken her ten minutes. Ten minutes was up an hour ago when the other associates had all headed out for happy hour. *Woo-hoo*.

Two days ago, Brent's world had fallen apart. And hers had almost gone with it. Whether she was suffering from some post-traumatic stress, a broken heart or a combination of both, she didn't know, but her entire body hurt. Physically and emotionally.

Tears bubbled up and she shook her head. No. No more crying. Never in her life had she cried this much. She loved this man, without a doubt, but she wouldn't be the whipping girl because he refused to face the hurt and anger he'd buried. That, he'd have to do on his own. She was more than willing to help him, any day, any time, but he had to own up to it. Something he refused to do.

Penny's head popped over the top of the short cubicle wall. "Hey. You're here late. What are you working on?"

Jenna blinked away her tears and looked up. "Expense reports."

Whatever Penny saw on Jenna's face, she didn't like it. "Oh, no. What is it? Do you need to talk about what happened?"

God, yes. But that included talking about Brent, and

Brent was Penny's friend, too. Somehow, it didn't seem fair to him. "I'm okay."

Penny wheeled a chair over from one of the other desks and sat beside Jenna, gently rubbing her back. "Clearly, you're not."

Jenna swiped at her wet eyes. "He's so quick to blame me."

"Brent? For the other day? He *blamed* you for his cousin going nutso?"

Jenna gasped. "Of course not."

"Whew. You scared me. I couldn't imagine him doing that."

"He wouldn't. He just…" Jenna stared at the cubicle wall in front of her, focusing on the picture of her niece and her adorable toothless grin.

"What?"

She swirled her open hands in front of her chest. "He has all this pain and he won't deal with it. And the minute he starts to get emotionally attached, he figures out a way to end it because he doesn't want to get hurt. He used the case to push me away. Every time I did something he thought I shouldn't have done, he went off on me before asking me about it. And I know it's because he's afraid of the emotional fallout. I won't deal with him doing that. It's too hurtful."

"I'm sorry."

"Me, too."

"Has he called?"

Jenna finally sat back and spun her chair to face Penny. "Yes. Several times. I can't talk to him right now. Unless he's going to deal with his emotions, there's nothing to say. I can't live like this, constantly worrying something I do will make him run. It's not fair. To either of us."

The stitches on her face itched and she reached up, pressed on the bandage. *No scratching.* "And these damned stitches are driving me crazy. I just want to rip them out so I can see what my face will wind up being."

After everything that had happened, her face, her no-fail tool to getting her job done, might be permanently scarred. Now instead of seeing a pretty brunette, people would see a scarred one. All because she wanted to prove she was good at her job by cracking a cold case. And look what it had gotten her.

"It doesn't matter," Penny said.

Jenna glanced up, met her gaze. "What?"

"Your face. I know you think you're good at your job because of how you look. Maybe it helps, sure, but your investigative skills and your instincts are what make you good. I promise you that. Frankly, you solved this case and your looks had nothing to do with it."

Jenna cocked her head.

"Yes," Penny said. "I'm right. You didn't solve this case by falling back on low-cut shirts. Accept it."

Holy cow. She thought back. From that first day, it had been all about chasing leads, figuring out what had been missed, discovering evidence. She'd even chosen more conservative clothing after Brent had told her how smart she was.

She let out a strangled laugh. "This is horrible. It took me getting my heart ripped out to realize I'm good at my job and it's not about my boobs."

"No, it's not. And I think you and Brent have a lot to talk about. Maybe you should call him back. See where this thing goes. Obviously, you care about each other."

"I care too much. That's the problem. We're stuck. And until he's ready to make changes, we'll stay that way."

With that, Jenna sat forward, covered her face with her hands and finally let the tears fall.

BRENT STOOD IN the now-empty living room of his child-hood home staring at the wood floor where his mother had died. All the years he'd lost with her crashed down on him and he sucked in a breath.

No doubt, the house, the memories, all of it had tormented him and altered the course of his life. Made him hard inside. Hard and alone. Sure he had his family, what was left of it anyway, but for himself? Nothing. Nada. For years he'd chosen to be the lone wolf. Now, with his family blown apart, he envied his sister for the life she'd built and found solace in. His life had been his mother's case.

And look where that had gotten him.

Outside, a car door slammed and he wandered to the door, his insides grinding like rusty gears. His own fault for burying his agony. When he got to the doorway, he glanced back at the living room. This was it. He had to let it go. Let his mother go. How he'd do it, he wasn't sure, but he had a starting point.

He hoped.

Brent stood with his feet just inside the threshold. *Go.* The porch was right there, the overhang blocking the bright sunshine. If he stepped out now, that would be it. Thousands of times he'd left this house. Today would be different. Today he had answers.

"Brent?"

Jenna stood at the base of the stairs in jeans tucked into boots, and wearing a flowy white shirt and a black leather jacket.

He'd called her each day for the last three days, but her only response had been a text telling him she'd call him soon. Which she hadn't yet done. Couldn't blame her. He'd shoved her away enough. Now he had to throw himself on her mercy.

And alter his plan of attack.

"Hi," he said.

"Hi."

"Thanks for coming."

"Your text said it was important."

"It is. How's your head?"

She shrugged. "Not bad. Still hurts a little."

She started to climb the steps, but he held up his hand. "I'm coming out."

And he did. He stepped over that threshold and—*how about that?*—it wasn't the torture he expected. Really, the only thing he felt was…relief.

He turned, closed the door behind him and met her at the bottom of the stairs.

"You didn't lock it," Jenna said.

"Don't need to."

"You're going back in?"

"No."

She stared up at him, her normally sparkly blue eyes flat, and that punch to the chest he always got made him realize all over again that he had major work to do. "I'm sorry."

"For what?"

"All of it. Pushing you away when you wanted to help. Firing you because I was scared. I'm a mess and you figured that out."

"Everyone is a mess, Brent. If everyone were perfect, life would be boring. The trick is to find people who accept the mess. I accept your mess. What I can't deal with is you taking your mess out on me. And, frankly, we could have talked about this in Chicago. Why drag me out here?"

He waved a hand toward the house. "I cleaned everything out."

"The house?"

"Yeah. It's empty."

She reached for him, squeezed his wrist and that feeling, that connection, shot clear up his arm. He wanted her. Even the high-maintenance parts that would drive him insane because she'd always want to talk. Talk. Talk. Talk. But he wanted it. All of it.

"Why?"

"It's over now. Did Russ tell you?"

She nodded.

"Sixteen women so far. That's the number they know about. Over twenty-three years, who knows how many more my uncle killed while on his road trips." He tipped his head back, let the sun warm his face and chase the chill from his body. "He doesn't even know why he did it. It's…"

"Twisted," Jenna said.

"Yeah."

"I'm so sorry."

Jenna wasn't the only one. "I don't know where we all go from here."

"How's Sylvie?"

"She's in Florida. Camille and I forced her to go visit her friend. We're hoping she stays a while. Right now, there's no reason for her to be here. Her daughter and her husband are in custody. Her family was blown apart too, and as bad as this situation is for Camille and me, as broken as we are, I can't even go where my aunt has to. How the hell does someone recover from that?"

Jenna sighed. "I wish I knew."

On the road, a flatbed carrying an excavator came to a whooshing stop, and Brent used his free hand to wave.

Jenna angled back. "What's with the tractor?"

"That's why you're here."

"Pardon?"

He pulled his wrist loose and grabbed both of hers. "We're tearing it down."

She made a tiny gasping noise. He'd surprised her. Good.

"I don't understand."

"The house. It's coming down. We talked to my dad. We reminded him he walked out and, for once, he needed to do what Camille and I wanted. That shut him up."

Jenna continued to gawk at him. "He *agreed* to this?"

"After I told him I'd handle selling the property and would give him the money. He can have it. I don't care. I want it over. I need a life."

"Are you sure you're ready for this? It's awfully fast."

"Twenty-three years is fast?"

She squeezed his hands. "You know what I mean."

He smiled. "Yeah, I do."

"So, your father is gone again?"

"Left yesterday. Probably better that way. At least I have his number. He said he'd call me. We'll see. I'm not counting on anything. Maybe I'd like to try talking once in a while. We'll never be close, but…I don't know. I guess I need to tell him how angry I am that he walked out." He waved it off. "Anyway, I'm tearing this house down and I wanted you here. Not because I couldn't do it alone, because I can."

"I know you can. You, Marshal Thompson, can do anything you set your mind to."

Hopefully, she truly believed that. He squeezed her hands again. "I'm ready. I thought letting this house go would be the hardest thing I'd ever do, but it's not. And, hold on to your beauty-queen panties because I'm about to say something that will blow your mind."

She rolled her eyes. "Uh-oh."

"No uh-oh. I hope—*I hope*—you'll be happy. Or at least open to it because letting this house go isn't the hardest thing I've ever done. These last few days without you made me realize that letting you go is worse. Way worse. And it hurts. Every time I see you I get this crazy banging in my chest. At first, it baffled me. Now, I think it's my mother poking me, telling me you're the one. Even if I didn't want to admit it in the beginning, I know it now, and I'm asking you to let me try again. To make this right. And I'm starting with tearing this house down. It's an albatross and—"

"Stop talking."

Come again? Always begging him to talk and now she wanted him to shut up. Women. "You want me to stop?"

"Yes."

This didn't sound good. Too late. That had to be it. She was done and, if he knew anything, he knew what that felt like. When he was done with something, it was over, no going back. Ever.

"So, you're done?"

"With?"

"Uh, me?"

"Why would you think that?"

And—hell in a handbasket—could he get a break here? Relationships being the last thing he understood was not helping him. At all. He breathed deep. "Because you told me to stop. Generally that indicates something is over."

"You don't have to skin yourself for me. All I want is for you to be honest. If it means not talking, fine. But don't use excuses to bury what you're feeling. I won't hurt you and I won't think you're weak. I need you to deal with your emotions, though. That's the only way we'll survive."

He nodded. "Leave it to me to find a psychology major."

She snorted. "A psychology major who loves you."

She loved him. Somewhere in his miserable life he'd become the luckiest guy walking. The stress of the last few days dropped from his body. Just gone. He stood for a second, for once, not stressing. About anything.

"I love you, Brent. And I want us to have a life together. I think it would be a good life. I know what I need, and I think I know what you need. But you have to know, too. You have to meet me halfway and not close up on me all the time."

He could do it. Surprise, surprise. Typically, if a woman had said that to him, he'd have made his exit. Now, not only did he believe he could do it, he wanted to do it.

"I can do that. It won't happen overnight, though. I've

spent years conditioning myself. But, I'll make it happen. I have to." He gestured to the house. "This is no way to live. I need a life. And I want you in it. I think I've loved you from the second I saw you in Penny's hallway. You see beyond the nonsense. I mean, you're a pain in the neck sometimes, and you definitely broke our agreement by coming out here and chasing after my Dad alone."

"I know. I'm sorry. I thought if your aunt or uncle were here it would be okay. I didn't think it through." She tugged on his shirt. "I didn't think like you would."

He shrugged. "You're bold. Sometimes, I like that about you. *Sometimes*."

She rolled her eyes, but ruined it with a grin. "So romantic."

Then he kissed her, brushing his lips slowly over hers, taking it all in and enjoying the connection. Jenna created chaos, he'd always known that, but her chaos was the good kind. The healing kind.

"Ahem."

He backed away. The truck driver shuffled behind Jenna, checking out her rear. Brent imagined he'd have to get used to that.

"Hi," he said to the guy. "In case you're wondering, she's mine."

Jenna cracked up. "Ooh, cave man. Nice."

"This the right address?" the guy asked, ignoring Brent's comment.

"Yep," Brent said. "We're knocking down this house."

"Okay."

That simple. If this guy only knew. He lumbered off and Brent turned back to Jenna. "Will you stay with me? Watch it go down? Then we'll leave. The cleanup might be too much, but the going down part, I need to see it."

She grabbed hold of his hand, linking her fingers with

his and snuggled into him. "I'll stay. Then we'll go some-where and, I don't know, just have quiet time, I guess."

Quiet time with Jenna. He'd like that. "Thank you."

"Sure."

"Not for staying. For not giving up on me. For forcing me to bust out of that stupid emotional cage. You could have walked away and you didn't. For that, I'll love you forever."

* * * * *

COMING NEXT MONTH FROM

H HARLEQUIN

I N T R I G U E

Available January 20, 2015

#1545 CONFESSIONS
The Battling McGuire Boys • by Cynthia Eden
Framed for murder, Scarlett Stone is desperate and turns to private investigator—and her former lover—Grant McGuire for help. If Grant is going to keep Scarlett at his side and in his bed, he has to stop the killer on her trail...

#1546 HEART OF A HERO
The Specialists: Heroes Next Door
by Debra Webb & Regan Black
Specialist Will Chase and trail guide Charly Binali race through the Rockies to stop a national security threat. When a single misstep could be their last, Charly must trust her life and her heart to this handsome stranger.

#1547 DISARMING DETECTIVE
The Lawmen • by Elizabeth Heiter
FBI profiler Ella Cortez's hunt for a rapist takes her to the Florida marshes, into the arms of homicide detective Logan Greer, and into the path of a cunning killer. Falling in love could be deadly...or the only way to survive...

#1548 THE CATTLEMAN
West Texas Watchmen • by Angi Morgan
Cattleman Nick Burke and DEA agent Beth Conrad are opposites—but they have to fake an engagement to trap gunrunners on Nick's ranch. Will they overcome their differences to close the case and find a love that is all too real?

#1549 HARD TARGET
The Campbells of Creek Bend • by Barb Han
Border Patrol agent Reed Campbell finds Emily Baker hiding out in a crate of guns smuggled into Texas. He knows keeping her safe will be hard—but keeping his hands to himself might be nearly impossible...

#1550 COUNTERMEASURES
Omega Sector • by Janie Crouch
Omega agent Sawyer Branson was sent to safeguard Dr. Megan Fuller while she neutralized a dangerous weapon that had fallen into enemy hands. Can Sawyer protect her long enough to finish the countermeasure, or will he have to choose between his agency and his heart?

YOU CAN FIND MORE INFORMATION ON UPCOMING HARLEQUIN® TITLES, FREE EXCERPTS AND MORE AT WWW.HARLEQUIN.COM.

HICNM0115

REQUEST YOUR FREE BOOKS!
2 FREE NOVELS PLUS 2 FREE GIFTS!

H HARLEQUIN®

INTRIGUE®

BREATHTAKING ROMANTIC SUSPENSE

YES! Please send me 2 FREE Harlequin Intrigue® novels and my 2 FREE gifts (gifts are worth about $10). After receiving them, if I don't wish to receive any more books, I can return the shipping statement marked "cancel." If I don't cancel, I will receive 6 brand-new novels every month and be billed just $4.74 per book in the U.S. or $5.24 per book in Canada. That's a savings of at least 14% off the cover price! It's quite a bargain! Shipping and handling is just 50¢ per book in the U.S. and 75¢ per book in Canada.* I understand that accepting the 2 free books and gifts places me under no obligation to buy anything. I can always return a shipment and cancel at any time. Even if I never buy another book, the two free books and gifts are mine to keep forever.

182/382 HDN F42N

Name _____ (PLEASE PRINT)

Address _____ Apt. #

City _____ State/Prov. _____ Zip/Postal Code

Signature (if under 18, a parent or guardian must sign)

Mail to the **Harlequin® Reader Service:**
IN U.S.A.: P.O. Box 1867, Buffalo, NY 14240-1867
IN CANADA: P.O. Box 609, Fort Erie, Ontario L2A 5X3
Are you a subscriber to Harlequin Intrigue books
and want to receive the larger-print edition?
Call 1-800-873-8635 or visit www.ReaderService.com.

* Terms and prices subject to change without notice. Prices do not include applicable taxes. Sales tax applicable in N.Y. Canadian residents will be charged applicable taxes. Offer not valid in Quebec. This offer is limited to one order per household. Not valid for current subscribers to Harlequin Intrigue books. All orders subject to credit approval. Credit or debit balances in a customer's account(s) may be offset by any other outstanding balance owed by or to the customer. Please allow 4 to 6 weeks for delivery. Offer available while quantities last.

Your Privacy—The Harlequin® Reader Service is committed to protecting your privacy. Our Privacy Policy is available online at www.ReaderService.com or upon request from the Harlequin Reader Service.

We make a portion of our mailing list available to reputable third parties that offer products we believe may interest you. If you prefer that we not exchange your name with third parties, or if you wish to clarify or modify your communication preferences, please visit us at www.ReaderService.com/consumerschoice or write to us at Harlequin Reader Service Preference Service, P.O. Box 9062, Buffalo, NY 14269. Include your complete name and address.

HII3R

SPECIAL EXCERPT FROM

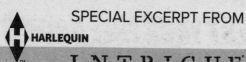

HARLEQUIN

INTRIGUE®

Read on for an excerpt from
CONFESSIONS, the first installment in
THE BATTLING McGUIRE BOYS *series*
by New York Times *bestselling author Cynthia Eden*

Framed for murder, Scarlett Stone turns to the only man
who can prove her innocence, private investigator
Grant McGuire—the man who broke her heart years ago.
If Grant is going to keep Scarlett at his side and in his bed,
he has to stop the killer on Scarlett's trail…

"I need you," she told him as she wet her lips. "I'm desperate, and without your help…I don't know what's going to happen." She glanced over her shoulder, her nervous stare darting to the door.

"Scarlett?" Her fear was palpable, and it made his muscles tense.

"They'll be coming for me soon. I only have a few minutes, and please, *please* stick to your promise. No matter what they say."

He shot away from his desk, his relaxed pose forgotten as he realized that Scarlett wasn't just afraid. She was terrified. "Who's coming?"

"I didn't do it." She rose, too, and dropped her bag into her chair. "It will look like I did, all the evidence says so…but I didn't do it."

He stepped toward her, touched her and felt the jolt slide all the way through him. Ten years…*ten years*…and it was still there. The awareness. The need.

Did she feel it, too?

Focus. "Slow down," Grant told her, trying to keep his voice level and calm. "Just take it easy. You're safe here." *With me.*

But that wasn't exactly true. She was in the most danger when she was with him. Only Scarlett had never realized that fact.

"Say you'll help me," she pleaded. Her tone was desperate. She had a soft voice, one that was perfect for whispering in the dark. A

HIEXP0115

voice that had tempted a boy…and sure as hell made the man he'd become think sinful thoughts.

"I'll help you," Grant heard himself say instantly. So he still had the same problem—he couldn't deny her anything.

Her shoulders sagged in apparent relief. "You've changed." Then her hand rose. Her fingers skimmed over his jaw, rasping against the five o'clock shadow that roughened his face. They were so close right then. And memories collided between them.

When she'd been eighteen, he'd always been so careful with her. He'd had to maintain his control at every moment. But that control had broken one summer night, weeks after her eighteenth birthday…

I can still feel her around me.

"Grant?"

She wasn't eighteen any longer.

And his control—

He heard voices then, coming from the lobby.

"Keep your promise," Scarlett said.

What the hell?

He pulled away from her and walked toward the door.

Those voices were louder now. Because they were…shouting for Scarlett?

"Scarlett Stone…!"

"They were behind me." Her words rushed out. "I knew they were closing in, but I wanted to get to you."

He hated the fear in her voice. "You're safe."

"No, I'm not."

Find out what happens next in
CONFESSIONS
by New York Times *bestselling author*
Cynthia Eden, available February 2015 wherever
Harlequin Intrigue® books and ebooks are sold.

Copyright © 2015 by Cynthia Roussos

HIEXP0115

JUST CAN'T GET ENOUGH?

Join our social communities
and talk to us online.

You will have access to the latest
news on upcoming titles and special
promotions, but most importantly,
you can talk to other fans about your
favorite Harlequin reads.

Harlequin.com/Community

f Facebook.com/HarlequinBooks

t Twitter.com/HarlequinBooks

P Pinterest.com/HarlequinBooks

HSOCIAL

JUST CAN'T GET ENOUGH
ROMANCE
Looking for more?

Harlequin has everything from contemporary, passionate and heartwarming to suspenseful and inspirational stories.

Whatever your mood, we have a romance just for you!

Connect with us to find your next great read, special offers and more.

Facebook.com/HarlequinBooks
Twitter.com/HarlequinBooks
HarlequinBlog.com
Harlequin.com/Newsletters

HARLEQUIN®

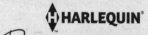
A Romance FOR EVERY MOOD™

www.Harlequin.com

SERIESHALOAD